THUGLIT

Issue Four

Edited by Todd Robinson

THUGLIT

THUGLIT: Issue Four
ISBN-13: 978-1482664546
ISBN-10: 1482664542

Stories by the authors: ©Roger Hobbs, ©Sam Wiebe, ©Anton Sim, ©Albert Tucher, ©Christopher Irvin, ©Eric Beetner, ©Garrett Crowe, ©Patti Abbott

Published by THUGLIT Publishing

Table of Contents

A Message from Big Daddy Thug   1

Through The Perilous Night by Anton Sim   3

Going In Style by Eric Beetner   15

Bet It All On Black by Christopher Irvin   33

Brass by Roger Hobbs   41

Under The Bus by Albert Tucher   51

Gallows Point by Sam Wiebe   67

Allure Furs by Patti Abbott   81

Of Being Darker Than Light by Garrett Crowc   93

Author Bios   109

THUGLIT

A Message from Big Daddy Thug

Welcome back, Thugketeers.

Big Daddy here, welcoming you back to the only literary magazine that you probably have to hide from your mom.

Been a busy time here at Casa de Thug, what with the launch of my novel THE HARD BOUNCE and such...

Actually, that's about it.

Feels like I should have more to say...

(ahem)

WELL, I don't. It's 3:30am, I'm about to eat some four-day-old roast beef stuffed into a stale everything bagel, and I'm trying to get this thing together for your beady little eyes to feast on.

Why, you ask? Why Big Daddy, do you risk both sanity and sleep for us, the faithful Thugketeers?

Because we love, THAT'S why. (*Ed. note*—love is that thing that makes you pee blood and have sleep-deprived hallucinations about spider-bagels with my third-grade teacher's face, right?)

LOVE, I SEZ!!!!

IN THIS ISSUE OF THUGLIT

- Ain't no party like a bankrupt party, cuz bankrupt parties don't…well, they do have to stop. There's no money left.
- No school like the really, *really*, old school.
- Don't gamble with this girl.
- Brass knuckles and brass balls. I wouldn't like either one to the face.
- Whores and politicians. One's at least honest, and it ain't the one that rhymes with *moliticians*.
- Old maaaan take a look at my life, killed a lot like youuuu. (apologies to Neil Young…)
- That fur isn't the only thing getting sold.
- A Harley and an open road can only get you so far.

See you in 60, fuckos!!!

Todd Robinson (Big Daddy Thug)
2/27/13

Through the Perilous Night
by Anton Sim

She found him in the small bedroom in the attic. He was lying in bed wearing his sneakers and watching *My Name is Earl* on TV.

"I didn't think anybody watched that," she said. "Except me."

"Nobody did. That's why they canceled it."

"It was pretty funny sometimes." Behind her, the sound of the party rumbled up from below, loud music and raucous laughter competing for supremacy. Colored lights reflected in the hallway, silhouetting her in a disco kaleidoscope.

"Let me guess," he said. "You like *Harold and Kumar* too."

"As a matter of fact I do. What does that tell you about me?"

"That you've got my sense of humor."

She polished off her drink and leaned on the antique dresser to watch the TV. "I'm going to ruin it for you," she said. "The season ends with a cliffhanger and they never come back."

"I know. Life stinks." He hit a button on the remote and the TV went blank.

"It's hot up here," she said, fanning herself. "Don't you think?"

"It's the top floor. Heat rises."

"You should open a window."

"I'm comfortable like this," he said.

"Nobody downstairs knows where you disappeared to. They said they hadn't seen you all night."

"Here I am."

"Here you are. You know, most hosts don't hide from their guests."

"Doesn't seem to be stopping them from enjoying the hospitality."

"Can I ask why you're holed up here instead of partying with your friends?"

"No you can't."

"Yes I can. Why aren't you downstairs?"

"I'm not feeling sociable. That's a hint."

"Well I figure it's only polite to introduce myself to the host," she said, extending her hand in greeting. "I'm Crystal."

"I know. You're kind of…unmistakable."

"Really? What gave it away?" Crystal didn't have an hourglass figure. Hers was a wineglass: thin at the stem and abundant up top.

"I've seen your work."

"What's that you're drinking?" She gestured.

"Booker's," he said, indicating the bottle cradled in the crook of his arm. "I keep hiding, booze keeps finding me."

"I'll take a hit of that," she said, holding out her empty glass.

"Harold, Kumar, Earl and bourbon. If I weren't feeling so misanthropic I'd call you a woman after my own heart." The bottle remained where it was.

"I've been called worse," she said, the glass still extended toward him. After a moment he relented and poured her a short slug.

"I'll bet you have. I don't want to be impol—"

4

Issue Four

"You know, you're kind of a legend around here, Jeremy," Crystal said, squirming onto the bed and making herself comfortable beside him.

He had to shift to make room for her. He didn't look happy about it. But he didn't look entirely unhappy either. "I'm not sure what that means."

"I got an condo in the Vandemark, up on Boulevard East. You know it?"

"No."

"Nice place, I like it, although you could fit my whole apartment in your garage. A couple of my friends up there told me about your parties. Your legendary parties, they called them."

"Is that right?" he said.

"Cheers," she said, clinking her glass against his. "And since this is supposed to be your last one, I figured it was now or never."

"My last one. You heard that, huh?"

"Word gets around."

"What else you hear?"

"Just what was on the news."

"Which was?"

Smiling, she sipped her bourbon. "Why you asking me?"

"Just curious. I don't watch the news."

She laughed. "Yeah, right. Well, I saw some of the interviews with Kyle Richmond. He puts all the blame on you as the segment producer. Says you cooked up the whole story, including the fake interviews and doctored tape, and you lied to him about it. He says he was just doing his job, reading off the teleprompter, and the only thing he did wrong was to trust you."

"Is that what he said?"

"He's obviously an airhead, so it's not entirely implausible he got conned, but he's also a conniving little bitch with the morals of a viper, and I think the viper part outweighs the airhead, so I don't buy his version."

"Meaning you think I'm innocent."

"Nobody's innocent, Jeremy. More bourbon, please."

He looked at her. She pouted, then slowly smiled, and he poured another finger of Booker's into her glass. "What else did you hear?"

"You are a masochist, aren't you? Well, I heard you found yourself in debt and wound up bankrupt."

"Bankrupt. Nice word. I was 'rupted by the bank," he said. "Have you ever been 'rupted, Crystal?"

"That sounds dirty."

"As a matter of fact, it is."

"Shit happens," she said. "Chapters end. New ones begin."

"Spoken like someone who's been down one or two bad roads in life."

"One or two," she agreed. "But I dusted myself off and started over and reinvented myself."

"With the aid of silicone?"

"As a matter of fact, yeah. With the aid of a lot of silicone."

"Since we're sharing a nice bottle of Booker's and a bed, can I ask you something, Crystal? Something I've always wondered about. Not about you specifically, but in general. How does it feel to fuck strangers for a living?"

"Bless my heart, you're trying to be rude. You know, if Kyle's telling even a teensy weensy bit of the truth, I could ask you that same question, Jeremy."

For the first time he laughed. Swigging directly from the bottle, he said, "Point goes to the lady."

"For some reason I pictured you older," she said. "The way you were described, it sounded like you'd been around the block."

"I've been around more blocks that you think. I'm just well-preserved."

Outside, a loud cheer rose from the houseguests.

"Sounds like the fireworks have started," Crystal said.

"Why don't you head downstairs to check it out?" he suggested.

"I've seen fireworks before."

"Not like this. You could sell this view for Broadway prices." From the balcony of the condo—one of a series of ritzy faux colonials perched on the lower banks of the Hudson River facing Manhattan—the Macy's Fourth of July display was practically overhead.

"This is fine," she said, sliding off the bed and wandering over to the dormer window. Sliding it open, she stuck her head out and said, "Omigod, this breeze is awesome. You should feel this."

"I'm comfortable," he said.

"Funny, you look sweaty."

The driving beat of the music was louder with the window open, as were the rowdy noises of the drunken revelers below. Leaning further out, Crystal could see onlookers crowded on the third-floor balcony below her, and the DJ with his huge speakers on the second-floor balcony below that, pounding out dance rhythms to drown out the patriotic music playing on neighbors' televisions and radios.

More of Jeremy's friends clustered together in small groups under strings of white lights in the backyard beside burning torches on wooden stands, refilling drinks at the bar, eating burgers and dogs from the grill manned by waiters in white shirts and bow ties. Beyond that, River Walk alongside the Hudson was crowded with partygoers leaning on the iron fence overlooking the river below, its black waves splashing against the rocky shoreline.

"Since we're getting all comfy and familiar, Jeremy, I want to ask you something too. I ask this whenever I meet anyone successful in their field. How did you get to be the person you are today?"

He took a sip and smacked his lips. "You know, I came up here tonight to be alone and I really don't want—"

"Fucking strangers for money can be easy-breezy like a paid vacation or it can be the most difficult job in the world," she said in answer to his earlier question. "It's all down to circumstances, meaning your partner, the crew, the location, the atmosphere, the weather, how much I partied the night before and if my allergies are acting up. Your turn."

He smiled. "I don't have a good answer for you, Crystal."

"Try. Tit for tat." She was staring at him coyly, her head tilted slightly to one side.

"You're a very persistent big-boobed person," he said.

"I am nothing if not that," she agreed.

"If I answer, will you go away?"

"I'm not used to be shooed away. It's kind of...beguiling. But yeah. If you want."

"Visualization," he said. "When I was young I made up my mind what I wanted to be and I focused all my energy on it and imagined myself rich. And I kept on imagining with all my heart—me with fancy cars, me with a Rolex for every day of the week, me with loads of dough and a wardrobe to die for, me with a killer condo like this one. And what do you know, here I am."

"All the material things," she said. "All the trappings. That's success in your book?"

"Of course. What else? Comfort, luxury, living the good life. That's what it's all about."

"Boring. Everybody craves the same stuff. The more stuff the better. Never enough stuff. Never fancy enough, never expensive enough. The ones with the best stuff walk around thinking they're better than everybody, with big, swelled heads."

"I'm going to assume that 'big, swelled heads' is a sexual innuendo," he said.

As if in punctuation, a loud crash came from downstairs. It sounded like some large, glass object had been broken. Several voices drifted upstairs, laughing.

"That can't be good," she said.

"Doesn't matter. It's the bank's now. I've been 'rupted, remember? Tell you what, on your way out, if you see anything you like, just take it with you. I'll report it stolen. Makes no difference anymore."

"Don't you think that's sad? Measuring yourself by what you own?"

"Time to go, Crystal. I answered your question."

"All that beautiful furniture downstairs, the antiques, those gorgeous Oriental rugs, the paintings, even that expensive booze I saw in the glass cabinet in the living room. I don't blame you for being proud of it. But doesn't it feel awful knowing it's all going away?"

"Nice talking to you. Bye."

"I'm not trying to put you down, Jeremy. Really, I'm not. Exactly the opposite. I think success is a matter of attitude. Don't focus on things, focus on yourself, who you are, who you want to be. Positive mental attitude; PMA. Happiness is what's important, not ownership."

"I'll keep that in mind."

"Take me, for example. I'm moving into legitimate acting, did you know that?"

"Crystal—"

"One of my first reviews said I had the 'freakshow appeal of two Jayne Mansfields stuffed in a single unitard.' Can you beat that?"

Despite himself, he laughed.

"But I didn't let it bring me down. I know who I am, I know what I'm capable of. I'm better than that. I just kept working, and you know what Richard Corliss said about me in *Dues and Don'ts*? He said I had the comedic chops of a young Carol Burnett. I'm going to take these out one day soon, you know." She hefted her breasts in her hands. "Once I'm established and people know me for my acting I won't need them anymore."

From outside came a series of booms loud enough to be heard over the music. The crowd cheered.

"Sounds like the climax," Jeremy said.

"Who's making with the sexual innuendo now?"

"It's been nice talking to you, Crystal. I wish you all the best in your boobless career, but you've really got to leave now. The fireworks are over, the party's going to wind down, everybody'll be going home. You've got to split."

"I get the hint; I'm going. Did I cheer you up any?"

"I'm so cheery I could shit. Have a good life, Crystal."

"I'm just going to tinkle and then I'll be on my way," she said, making for the bathroom.

"Downstairs, there's…" he began.

"I'll just be a sec, don't get your panties in a— *omigod.*"

She had pushed open the bathroom door and taken a step inside, then recoiled, her hand covering her mouth.

"*Omifuckinggod,*" she said.

"What is it?" he said, sliding off the bed to peer around her.

"Back off," she warned, moving fast, sliding against the wall. At the same time she snatched a small canister from a holster on her belt and held it up, pointed directly at him. "Don't come near me. This is mace."

"What are you—" Then he saw what was in the bathroom. A man in the tub, his head leaning on the rim above the pink water, his arm hanging over the edge, blood running in trails from his opened forearm into a darkening pool on the floor.

"Just stay away," she warned, edging toward the door.

"No, wait. Hold on. I didn't do that," he said, taking a step forward.

"Get the fuck away from me," she shouted, spraying a stream of mace. Throwing up his arms he managed to deflect the main blast, but a fine mist got past his hands. It felt like wire coat hangers had been jabbed into his eyes.

"I didn't even know he was in there," he yelled back, burning in pain, forcing himself not to rub his eyes and make it worse.

"Don't lie, Jeremy. That's why you were so anxious for me to leave."

"I'm not Jeremy. I was pretending."

"*Help!* Hey, somebody, anybody!" She was standing in the doorway, yelling down the stairs, still pointing the canister at him. "Call 911! Get the cops!"

Stumbling around the bed, he snatched up his knapsack from where he'd quickly stuffed it the moment he heard her coming up the stairs. Inside were some watches, rings and other jewelry he'd snagged in the master bedroom downstairs, plus a few other knickknacks that looked valuable. The front door had been open, people laughing and partying and hitting on each other, plucking food off silver trays and drinking liquor from the hired bar and paying no attention to strangers wandering in off the street. He hadn't been able to get much from the first two floors, crowded as they were with partygoers, but the third floor had been better and he had just begun ransacking the fourth when Crystal interrupted.

"I didn't do anything," he insisted, and a flash of insight came to him. "That must be Jeremy in the bathroom. He killed himself."

Nobody had seen Jeremy all night. That's what she said. Jeremy had invited everyone over, arranged for the liquor and the food and the DJ and the cooks and bartenders to be waiting, and then had gone upstairs and killed himself. His guests had breezed in and made themselves at home, boozing and carousing and enjoying the festivities, not knowing Jeremy's blood was soaking into the grout between the tiles above their heads. It was a gruesome joke, a spit in the face of propriety, a self-consciously ironic farewell from a man who'd lost everything.

"I didn't do it," he repeated, feeling like a rat in glue, standing with the half-empty knapsack gripped between bloodless fingers. The steely look on Crystal's face left no doubt as to whether she believed him.

Lifting the bag as a battering ram he charged for the door and bulled his way past her. Hurriedly scrambling backwards, she sprayed wildly and missed as he burst into the hallway, only to see three burly guys bounding up the stairs toward him.

No way was he going to make it past them. Instead he spun and headed back into the bedroom, slamming shut and locking the door.

"Don't touch me," Crystal hissed, sliding toward the corner with her back against the wall.

"I won't touch you," he snapped. "I won't come near you." There was only one way out. Throwing the knapsack over his shoulder, he began climbing out the window.

The balconies below were framed by decorative wrought iron railings. Easy to climb. A burglar's delight. Gripping the windowsill, he swung his legs down, searching with his feet for a purchase.

"Guess again," Crystal said, and when he instinctively looked up, she hit him full in the face with a blast of mace.

He knew better than to let go. But he couldn't help himself, with his flesh feeling like it was melting away from his skull, his eyes exploding in flame. His fingers lost their strength, lost their feeling, lost their grip. One foot caught in the iron railing and he flipped over, neatly snapping his shin and slamming the back of his head against the wall. Then as the foot slid free, he tumbled downward, bouncing off one of the speakers on the second floor balcony and landing facedown on the sizzling barbecue grill. A moment later the speaker landed on top of him, splintering his spine and crushing the grill to the patio stones like so much tinfoil.

In the sudden, glaring absence of pounding dance music, the sound of neighbors' radios and televisions could be heard echoing into the night, drifting out across the river, all tuned to the same station playing patriotic anthems as the smoke of the final, spectacular round of fireworks drifted down from overhead, blanketing the lawn like fog. Guests rushed madly for cover, knocking each other to the ground and trampling friends and strangers in their haste to escape whatever the hell was happening.

While upstairs in the bathtub, Jeremy grinned on.

THUGLIT

Going In Style
by Eric Beetner

"Seriously, fuck this place." Herb threw down the playing cards, scattering his gin rummy hand over the plastic table. The same deck they'd been playing with for two years—the one with two Queens of hearts and no red sevens. Herb ran a hand over his scalp, an old habit from when he sported an enviable head of hair. Now he clung to wisps of white on his skull and a dense new thicket of hair in his ears.

Charlie folded his cards neatly and laid them down, content to ride out another of Herb's rants. These days, Herb's temper was about the only entertainment at the Four Palms retirement home. He scratched his stubbly chin and pulled up the collar on his plaid flannel shirt. He could never seem to get warm anymore.

"I'm getting out," Herb said. "You hear me?" The question of hearing was a legitimate one around the home. As the population dwindled over the past few years due to die-out, the remaining residents constituted a lowly fifteen percent hearing ratio. Charlie wore a hearing aid, and he kept it cranked up so high he could hear a mouse fart.

"What are you gonna do when you're out?" Charlie asked, mostly to keep the conversation going now that the card game was over.

"I'll tell you what I'm gonna do. I'm gonna have some goddamn fun for a change, that's what."

About once every two months, Herb went on a tear about this and that around the home. The beds sucked—true. The food sucked—true. The selection of VHS tapes for them to watch sucked extra hard—true. The staff were trying to kill off the rest of the residents so they could close up shop and move on—unsubstantiated.

Herb's tantrums usually resulted in a night out—they were free to come and go—sometimes to a movie he and Charlie both fell asleep in. Charlie and Herb were best friends, but Charlie mostly went on the outings to keep Herb out of trouble. And Herb had a history of trouble.

When he described the circumstances around his arrival at the home, he split the description between accident and coincidence. But either way he told the story it still ended with him burning down his son's house, and after they built him a room over the garage and everything. After that, the wide-hipped Mexican lady his son married forced him into the Four Palms. Not that his boy—his only boy—wasn't complicit in a pussy-whipped sort of way. Maybe the lack of fire insurance gave the kid an extra reason to be cruel to his old man. Any way you slice it, Herb found himself dumped on the front step and they practically burned rubber out of parking lot.

When he and Charlie moved in during the same week two years ago, the Four Palms bustled with good-looking nurses, active residents and the sounds of jazzercise coming from the rec room. Now the whole place stank of death, both recent and impending. The staff had been replaced by more cost-effective employees. To Herb that meant people who could no more care for a human being than keep a houseplant from dying, and had all the bedside manner of a cactus with herpes. Plus, none of them spoke

English. At least not the way he wanted them to. Sounded a little too much like that daughter-in-law for his taste.

"So," Charlie said. "What's on the fun agenda this time?"

"Some real fucking fun for a change," Herb said.

"What's that mean?" Charlie wanted him to say strip club.

Herb stole a conspiratorial glance around the room, then dropped his voice low, even though no one could hear him anyway. Most of the fifteen percent who could hear were sitting at the table, and it was only him and Charlie. "It's no mystery we don't have much time left, right?"

Charlie nodded, curious about where this was going.

"So let's do something we don't have any more excuses not to do."

"What's that?"

"I'm going out and getting some heroin."

Charlie blinked. He wondered if he needed to turn up his hearing aid more. "Some what now?"

"You heard me, ya deaf old bastard." Herb showed yellow teeth as he grinned and nodded.

"I knew this day would come. You've gone off your rocker and now I need to find a new best friend. And look around you, who else am I gonna hang out with?" Charlie looked across the room where a man sat in a wheelchair parked in front of a potted plant, eyes glassy and a line of drool running off his chin and onto a knitted blanket in his lap.

"Listen, you," Herb said. "When I was in the service I had a two-week furlough in Singapore. While I was there I tried opium. I smoked it. Some guys I knew injected it too. I tell you what Charlie, it was the best damn feeling I ever had. It was heaven on earth and I've thought about that for more than sixty years since. Didn't hurt I had some teenaged girl working her magic on my tool. If I could pay that girl to suck me off again I would. But she's probably dead now, so heroin it is."

Charlie kept waiting for the joke. Herb stared him down. He seemed dead serious.

"How are you gonna get it?"

"We'll find a dealer?"

"Where?"

"Skid row."

Charlie blinked some more. He listened to the low mumble of the stereo playing the same mix tape running on infinite loop for the past decade. The songs, for those who can hear them, are a part of the ignored decor, like the peeling wallpaper or the dusty prints of sailboats and sunsets lining the walls like embalmed memories.

"You're serious."

"Damn straight I am." Herb leaned forward. "Now's the time, Charlie. When else in your entire life have you been able to honestly say it doesn't fucking matter what we do anymore? Haven't you always wanted to do some things? Let's see what all the fuss is about."

"Where are you gonna get the money?"

"I have some saved. Don't worry, I'll buy your share. I'd much rather spend it on living than buy another extra pudding cup with dinner."

Charlie had been thinking about death lately. About life lived and what he'd done and hadn't done. He couldn't say heroin was ever on his to-do list, but most of the things he regretted never getting to do, those opportunities were long gone.

"Go out with a bang, huh?" Charlie said.

"Might as well try everything once, right? Next week we'll go skydiving."

Charlie laughed until he coughed up a deep-seated ball of phlegm from the bottom of his lungs. He shook his head, not believing the words forming in his throat. "Okay, let's do it."

Issue Four

Herb clapped him on the shoulder, showing those yellow teeth again.

A female voice startled them from behind. "I want in."

Herb and Charlie turned to see Ruth, the only female resident left at Four Palms, and another member of the fifteen percent. As usual she wore a full-length dress, a relic from a bygone era when ladies wore pearls in the home.

"What are you talking about?" Herb said.

"Don't act like an idiot. I'm about the only other one who can hear a damn thing in this place and I heard all of it. I want to go with you." Ruth moved in five months ago and immediately joined forces with Herb and Charlie, two of the only mentally cogent people in the place. In her younger days she broke horses for a living, a profession that gave her, as she put it, "Brass balls bigger than both you boys. And let's not forget it."

"You ever try it before?" Herb asked.

"No, and I never fucked JFK either, but I'd do that in a second too if I had the chance. What do say?" Ruth said.

Charlie looked to Herb for approval.

"We leave tomorrow night."

*****

Ruth showed up at the door dressed for a cocktail party. Herb and Charlie dressed for a trip to the crapper.

Ruth maintained a vanity about her appearance. Despite being well north of 80 years old, she continued to dye her hair a jet black to match the photos of the younger self she kept on every flat surface of her room.

When he saw her, Charlie cinched up his sweatpants and smoothed his hair with his fingers.

"Where the hell do you think we're going?" Herb asked. "A goddamn debutante ball?"

"I'm going out, Herb. Doesn't matter where. A lady dresses to go out."

Herb shook his head. "The day I retired I took all my neckties and burned them in the back yard. Couldn't pay me to wear one of those chokers again."

"I think you look nice, Ruth," Charlie said.

"Thank you," Ruth said, smiling.

"Come on," Herb grumbled. "Let's go."

*****

To no one's surprise, the front desk was empty when they left. None of the staff would know they were gone.

Outside they met the taxi Herb called and all climbed in with a chorus of moans and creaking bones, like zombies crawling from the grave. Ruth sat in the middle, three sets of fragile hips pressed against each other.

"Where to?" the cab driver asked.

"Skid row," Herb said.

"What?"

"You heard me. Take us to the shittiest part of town."

"Why do you want to go there?"

"Why don't you mind your business?"

The cabbie shook his head and pressed a button to start the meter.

*****

No one spoke much during the drive until the neighborhood outside began to change and it became apparent their destination loomed.

"So," Charlie said. "How do we know who to ask?"

"They come to you," Herb said. "Don't you read the papers? There's drug dealers all over the place nowadays."

"Do you know how much to get?" Ruth asked.

"Enough for three. They'll know."

"And you said you did this before, right?" Ruth asked.

"Yeah. It was fantastic." Herb turned to look at Ruth. "Of course at the time there was a girl--"

"I heard all about that and you can forget it." She turned to the ugly streets outside.

"What happened to a 'what the hell' attitude about life?"

"I may be nearly dead, but I still have my standards. If you're so gung-ho to try something new, why not let Charlie blow you?"

Herb's mouth hung open as if he might say something, but nothing came out. Charlie coughed up another wad from his lung.

"Where should I stop?" the cab driver asked.

"Here is good," Herb said. He felt grateful for the excuse to leave the tight confines of the cab.

They got out on a corner in front of a clothing store with signs in Spanish and a sturdy roll cage covering the storefront after hours. Herb paid the cab driver.

"I ain't waiting around in this neighborhood," the cabbie said.

"Then fuck off." Herb gave him the finger as the cab drove away. He hadn't felt this young in years.

The trio couldn't have looked more out of place on the corner if they'd time-traveled.

"So where do we start?" Charlie asked.

"I guess we start walking," Herb said.

They moved as a pack, fear keeping them tightly bunched and walking slow. The people on the street stared. A car rolled by slowly on low-riding rims, blasting window-rattling bass from speakers filling the back seat.

In nearly every doorway was a cardboard shelter and a strong urine smell. Shopping carts were filled with the sum total of people's possessions.

None of the shops were open. Most of them looked to be closed for good. Ruth hooked an arm around Charlie's and held on tight.

"Let's try the park," Herb said.

Across the street was a patch of grass with three overhead lamps, two of which were burned out. A basketball court stood to the side of the park area, but the hoops had been removed. A body stretched out on a bench in a mound of dirt-crusted clothing.

"What the fuck is this?" said a young man from the shadows.

The trio of seniors stopped walking.

The man stepped out from the darkness. A young Latino, puffing on a thin cigar. White t-shirt over baggy jeans. Shaved head and several tattoos in a gothic font decorated his arms and neck. "You lost or something?"

Charlie and Ruth both looked to Herb as their leader.

"We're looking to buy."

The Latino pulled a deep lungful of smoke off the cigar. "Buy what?"

Herb swallowed. *Fuck it*, he thought. *This is living*. "Heroin."

The Latino man laughed, clouds of smoke chugged out above him. "Are you for real?"

"Yes."

"What the fuck do you want that for?"

Herb screwed up his courage and his newfound attitude and stepped forward. "Because I'm eighty-eight years old and I just don't give a fuck anymore. Now are you holding or what?"

The Latino man drew deep on the cigar again. He looked Herb over, then scanned up and down on Ruth and Charlie.

"No, I'm not holding," he said. "But I can get you some."

"When?"

"Tonight. I'll bring it to you."

"We can wait."

"No, no, man. That's no good. You hang out here and you'll be stripped and sold for parts faster than a Cadillac, man."

Ruth clutched tighter to Charlie.

Issue Four

"You tell me where to meet you and I'll bring the stuff. No extra charge."

Herb thought it over. Hadn't the whole night been a big chance? What's one more? He gave him the address.

"Herb," he said, introducing himself.

"Martin," the dealer said. "Give me two hours."

Charlie cleared his throat. "Do you know where we can get a cab?"

As Martin watched the lights of the gypsy cab turn the corner, he thought; *easy targets.* Too old to be cops. From the looks of it, she had money. But how much on her? Not enough to chance robbing them on his own corner.

As he'd given them his once-over, a plan began to form. Old folks had savings. Maybe old jewels and shit like that. If he could get to their place, it would be easy pickings. A good shove with his pinky finger and they'd fall down like that lady in the commercial who couldn't get up.

Yeah, this could be a good night.

*****

They waited in Herb's room. His roommate, Floyd, didn't care. He'd been hooked up to his machines for the night and hovered much closer to death than life. The oversized hospital bed dominated Herb's smaller, normal bed in the room. Floyd's upper body was elevated so he didn't choke on the mucus his lungs created during the night, and the adjustable bed was bent at the legs so he didn't throw a blood clot to his brain.

"You sure Floyd's not gonna wake up?" Charlie asked.

"Him?" Herb said. "He's nine toes in the grave. Don't worry about it."

Ruth kept watch at the window, her head behind the curtain. "He's here," she said.

23

Herb met Martin in the driveway. Once again, no one was at the front desk.

"You got it?"

"Yeah. Let's go inside." Martin looked over the exterior of the Four Palms. Not exactly the retirement palace he expected.

"I got the money right here." Herb went for his back pocket. Martin stepped forward and put a hand on his wrist.

"Yo, fool, don't go doing that out here in the open. This here is a drug deal, man. Let's go where we can have some privacy."

"The park where we found you is out in the open," Herb said.

"I know all the dudes around there. I don't know shit in this neighborhood. Now you want this or not?"

Herb led him inside.

Martin's face fell when he saw Floyd and all the apparatus. "What the fuck . . .?"

"Don't mind him," Herb said.

Charlie laid out three syringes they had acquired easily from the supply closet earlier, and a spoon lifted from the cafeteria.

Martin scanned the room, looking for where a safe might be.

Herb held out the money. "Here you go."

Martin took the stack of bills and handed over a wad of plastic wrap tied off with a rubber band. Inside was a dingy yellow powder. Ruth and Charlie exchanged a look, each one wondering if that is indeed what heroin looks like.

"You know what the fuck you're doing with that?" Martin asked.

"Yeah, sure." Herb had logged on to the computer in the rec room, the one still hooked in to a dial-up modem, and searched how to prepare and inject heroin. He came out with an alarming number of tutorials. He even found a YouTube video that only took forty-eight minutes to load.

"Ruth, light the candle," he said. Ruth brought a lighter out of her cardigan pocket and lit a small votive candle.

"You can go now," Charlie said to Martin.

"No, no. If it's all right with you, I'll hang around and watch this shit. Might be good."

Herb took the spoon and went to Floyd's bedside. He pulled the IV from his arm and dripped the liquid into the spoon.

Ruth said, "Herb!"

"It's saline. We need water and this is a pure as it gets. Relax, he won't miss it. Only ends up here in an hour anyway." Herb pointed to the dark yellow liquid in a catheter bag hanging off the side of Floyd's bed.

As Herb prepared the shot, Martin moved around the room, ignored by the three nervous seniors. He lifted picture frames, opened a bedside drawer by Herb's bed.

Herb drew up the first shot and turned to Charlie and Ruth. "Who's first?"

"Shouldn't it be you?" Charlie said. His voice trembled slightly, like a kid being asked to do something he knew broke the rules.

"I was gonna give you and Ruth the shots before I go. If you'd rather give yourself—"

"No." Charlie said, then he licked his dry lips. "Go ahead. I'll go." He could see the doubt and fear on Ruth's face. She smiled at him when their eyes met.

Herb lined up the needle with a vein. The skin gave way easily and a tiny bead of blood grew from the hole. Herb didn't ask, he pushed the plunger down and drew the needle out. Herb took Charlie's index finger and placed it over the new hole in his arm.

"Hold that there."

Herb and Ruth could see when the drug hit his brain. His eyelids fluttered, then dimmed to half-mast. A timid smile crept over his lips.

"Better get him in a chair," Herb said. He and Ruth guided Charlie to a seat. "Looks pretty happy, doesn't he?"

"Yeah, he does," Ruth agreed.

"This is nice and all," Martin said. "But where's the rest of the money?"

Herb and Ruth looked up to see Martin pointing a gun at them.

"I gave you the money," Herb said.

"The rest of what you got. I know that ain't all of it."

"What is going on?" Ruth asked.

"Shut up lady, you'll get your turn. Better have some nice jewelry and shit too. There's fuck-all in this room." Martin pushed forward, thrusting the gun at Herb's forehead. Martin bumped Charlie's knees as he moved. Charlie didn't care.

"I don't have any more money," Herb said.

"Bullshit!" The barrel of the gun pressed hard into Herb's skull.

"Okay, okay. I have a few more dollars. But that's all, I swear."

"Get it." Martin spoke in his best bad-guy-from-the-movies voice. "Then we get his and hers."

Herb swung out with his right hand. The needle caught Martin in the neck.

Ruth threw her hand up to cover her ears as Martin yelled. Martin slapped a hand to his neck and turned, ripping the syringe out of Herb's hand. Herb already slid his hand down Martin's tattooed arm and gripped the wrist above the gun. He spun Martin's wrist with sixty-year-old U.S. Marines training and had the arm pinned behind his younger attacker in a second.

Charlie moved his head like he was watching a tennis match, the look on his face unsure if this was real or the drug.

Issue Four

Herb shoved Martin and the drug dealer fought back. They tumbled across the room, Herb too afraid to let go. Martin's face bounced off the chrome railings on the side of Floyd's bed and Herb pushed down. As their bodies slid the length of the bed, Floyd's catheter bag caught on Martin's knees and came loose, spraying cold piss over the fight and onto the floor.

"Ruth, help me," Herb said. She stood still, in a panic.

Martin's head went down and Herb nearly rode up on his back. He could feel himself losing his grip on the younger man's arm. Carrying the old man's weight on his back pushed Martin forward and his head wedged in the opening where Floyd's bed was raised. Herb pushed harder to keep Martin's head in the small triangle of space, like a rat in a trap.

"Here, push," he said to Ruth, kicking out with his foot and sending the remote for the reclining bed to her. She lunged forward and grabbed the box swinging on the end of a cable. She got it in her hand and jammed the toggle forward with her thumb. The bed began to flatten.

Martin's screams became louder as the electric motor drove the bed frame closed around his neck. Herb wasn't sure how long he could hold the man there. His arms were already rubber and sweat rolled off his forehead. He thought of his drill sergeant barking insults over his shoulder, used the deeply ingrained Marine determination that never left his bones.

Ruth looked away, but kept her thumb on the button.

The motor ground and protested at the object blocking the way. Martin dropped the gun and it rattled on the linoleum floor. Floyd did not stir. No staff member came to the rescue.

"Cook another shot," Herb said to Ruth.

"What?"

"Cook another shot. Give him all of it." Herb dripped sweat onto Martin's back and into his own mouth. Ruth handed him the remote and he kept his thumb on the

27

toggle, despite the grinding motor. Martin's struggles were weakening.

Charlie tried to stand, took two steps and fell onto Herb's bed. He kept his fingers on his vein the entire time.

Ruth spit into the spoon, poured the rest of the powder in, heated the mixture over the candle the way she'd seen Herb do it, then uncapped a syringe and drew up as much of the liquid as she could.

By the time she turned, Martin stopped moving.

Herb huffed deep, struggling breaths. The bed's motor clicked in a steady rhythm, unable to move against the solid block of Martin's head. Ruth saw blood dripping beneath the bed mixing with the piss from the now-empty bag.

A deep retching sound came from across the room and Charlie leaned over the side of Herb's bed and vomited on the floor. He fell back into position on Herb's pillow.

"Do you still need this?" Ruth asked as tears formed in her eyes. She held the syringe out between them.

"No," Herb said between breaths. "I think we're okay."

"But he's . . ."

"Yeah."

Herb let go and bent down to pick up the gun. His arm could barely lift it.

"What now?" Ruth asked.

Herb looked around the room. The pool of blood, the spill of vomit, the syringe in her hand filled with piss-yellow liquid. The never-ending pulse of Floyd's breathing apparatus droned on.

"We clean up."

*****

Forty minutes later the room was disinfected and mopped cleaner than it had been in years. Charlie curled in a ball on Herb's bed, asleep and twitching every now and then.

Martin's body was rolled in a sheet on the floor, looking like a giant cocoon. They used one of the sheets with a rubber barrier against bed wetting. It kept the blood pooled inside and away from their spotless floor.

Herb took a moment and leaned against the dresser. He watched Floyd as the machines breathed for him, drained the piss from him, and kept the reaper at bay. The old bastard with the scythe had to settle for a substitute this night.

"What do we do with him?" Ruth asked.

"We could dump him in Roy's old room," Herb said.

Roy kicked off last month. Natural causes, they said. The ones who could hear would tell you he called out to the staff for an hour that night. When he finally went quiet everyone assumed he gave up. In a way, he did.

"Won't they find him?" Ruth said.

"Yeah, that's no good." Herb ran his hand over his head, his scalp clammy with sweat. Another day in this hellhole and it's gone shittier than usual. And all he wanted to do was have some fun, just like the night of the fire. Can't an old man enjoy a goddamn cigar anymore? Was it his fault he fell asleep? Was it his fault they didn't have a goddamn fire extinguisher?

Ask his son and he'd say yes. That bitch of a wife would say *Si*.

"I got an idea," Herb said.

*****

Distracting the cab driver had been fairly easy for Ruth. She let the men get the "luggage" while she explained where they were headed. Getting Charlie awake enough to help stuff the mummy wrapped body in the trunk had been harder.

He moved underwater-slow, his eyes always at risk of falling shut. They let him sit against the open window as they drove in case he needed to puke again, and maybe the cold air would sober him up.

When they pulled up in front of the address the cab driver asked, "This is where you want to go?"

Herb said yes and made Ruth pay the man as he and Charlie retrieved the luggage.

Two years on and the house was still nothing more than a pile of old cigar ash. The char-blackened chimney bricks still stood, so did much of the back porch, but the bones of the house stuck out of a charcoal pit like a dozen burnt matchsticks shoved into the earth.

The cab pulled away and they dragged Martin's wrapped and ready body into the pile of ash, smoothed over a coating of camouflage to last at least until the next rain.

They all stepped back to the sidewalk, clapping soot from their hands. They turned to face the nonexistent house.

"You did this, huh?" Ruth asked.

"Yeah," Herb said, examining the full extent of the damage for the first time. "I guess I did." He really had fucked up bad. Damn good thing they didn't have kids. "What a fuckin' mess," Herb said.

Ruth put a hand on his arm and Herb ran his eyes over the pile of nothingness. Herb told himself to call his son and apologize in the morning. And to finally learn his daughter-in-law's name.

"Look at me," Charlie said. Herb and Ruth both turned. Charlie had taken soot from the pile and given himself an Al Jolson blackface. His teeth practically glowed white as he smiled against his pitch black face.

"Oh, brother," Herb said. He and Ruth got on either side of Charlie and escorted him back to the Four Palms. They were all out of cab fare.

Issue Four

They returned to Herb's room ninety minutes later and each breathed a deep sigh of relief. By then Charlie had mostly sobered up, but seemed overcome by tiredness.

"Should we get Charlie to his own bed?" Ruth asked.

"No, don't bother. I'll take his." Herb guided Charlie to his own bed and let him collapse.

Ruth noticed the syringe lying on the dresser top. Herb saw it too.

"After all this," Ruth said. "Do we?"

"It was a hell of a lot of trouble to go through with nothing to show for it."

"I wouldn't say nothing. You got your excitement."

"Not in the way I planned."

"You mean not the way you remember."

"That too."

Ruth eyed the needle. "Was it really that good?"

Herb smiled. "I'm still thinking about it after all this time."

Ruth lifted the syringe and held it out to him. "Do you think it will be the same without the blowjob?"

"Probably not, but I'm willing to try."

"Well," Ruth said, pushing up the sleeve of her sweater. "Maybe we can do something about that."

Bet It All On Black
by Christopher L. Irvin

When the last tiny air bubble escapes Tom's mouth, rising wobbly to the surface and then popping with a *splick*, my face flushes as his abs grow taut underneath my ass and heat ripples up my spine. It feels wrong—so much that I taste sour in my throat—but I can't hide the smile stretching across my face. The pleasurable tingle changes to spiders crawling, laying goose bumps under my skin and I shudder. It scares me how much I enjoy the moment, that the space where I should feel sharp pangs of fear and regret is dull and numb. And it's not the first time.

I sit on his stomach, letting my pale, one hundred-twenty-pound frame hold him under for a few more seconds to ensure he's gone. Even though the bathwater is almost boiling I feel cold, like a professional behind a computer screen, watching Tom drown at the push of a button. I step out of the tub before he fouls himself.

Tom had said it was the best room in the casino and he wasn't kidding. Water is splattered all over the granite tile. The sink, a mess of towels and toiletries, made it look like Tom had been living in the place for a week, when in reality it was the obsessive need of a drunk man to unpack before inviting me, his guest, into the suite. All it did was make it look like I had wrestled him out of a week's worth of Tommy Bahama before drowning him in the tub. Surrounded by luxury, and all I can think of is the mess.

The bathroom is almost as large as my apartment, the whirlpool tub at its center. I say "my apartment" but it was really Doug's place, and now it belongs to the bookies along with everything else I used to own—with the exception of the six-inch silver heels, the purse and the black strapless dress laying on the bed in the other room. Not my style, but every girl has an outfit for when she's looking for trouble.

The long beveled mirror above the double sink is fogged over, and in the haze of the steam-filled room I feel a strange sense of calm. It reminds me of when I was thirteen, when Doug capped The Streak of '03, winning a gunmetal Mustang convertible at The Mirage. He pulled me out of school and drove us from Vegas to LA, his lucky pockets full of cash winnings. We hit the basin fog and just rolled on through to the coast. Doug wasn't sober for a second of that long weekend, but I didn't care. I was his daughter.

That was the last time I knew where I was going in life. Doug's winning streak came to an end shortly after the trip. He rarely came home at night, and when he did, he reeked of sweat and booze or a woman's perfume, only stopping by for a shower and a change of clothes, or to argue with the landlord over late rent. I learned to take care of myself and kept my father locked inside my heart next to a faded photograph of my dead mother. Doug told me nothing other than she died having me. I don't know if I believe him, but he named me Mirna after her. He called me Mirn when he had something to say, which was hardly ever towards the end.

Tom had called me Mirn too. If there had been anything heavier than a hairdryer in the bathroom I would have beaten him to death. But I gritted my teeth as I stripped off my dress and tied my hair back into a short, tight ponytail. I teased Tom into the tub filled to the brim with screaming hot water. I giggled when I knocked him in and the water scalded his skin. But Tom was not as drunk as I thought he was. That, or his adrenaline overcame the combination of heat and the half-bottle of Bulleit he downed after stumbling to the hotel room less than an hour before. I thought about wiping down the walls but they would dry, leaving little sign of struggle. It's not like I slashed his aorta and he sprayed crimson all over the bathroom.

Not like my father.

I picked Tom out of the crowd around one of the many craps tables at the Bellagio. I'd just dropped off three thousand to the bookie's men and received a black eye for the effort. I hadn't stepped foot on a casino floor in years, and yet I'd been on two in less than twenty-four hours. I felt the family itch coursing through my veins, an addiction not only to the game, but the environment, the shows, the crowds. All gilded over a rotten core.

In five minutes of my eyeing him from across the table and cheering with the raucous crowd, he had won over three grand. Tom was well into his fifties. His voice hinted at years of smoke-filled rooms, and when I squeezed in close to him, he smelled of cheap body spray and bourbon. He handed me a free Jack and Diet from a cart, clinking glasses. Cocking his head to the side, he put a hand on my lower back and told me my black eye was cute in a "you remind me of my daughter" kind of way. His eyes crinkled when he smiled. He could have been a father of five but I convinced myself he was a bad man. Tom had won over twenty grand last night and the casino had given him one of their top suites for the remainder of the week. Three hours later, I had him drunkenly cashing chips and heading for the room.

I feel the night of free drinks squirm in my stomach as I stand dripping in the bathroom. For a brief moment I feel faint and need to brace myself on the counter as the scene takes its toll. Tom's lifeless body reminds me of

Doug, minus the slashed wrists and blood. Doug had done it right—doped himself up and taken a pair of my nice scissors deep and horizontal—not like the paper cuts you see in the movies. I found him three days ago on a scorching Friday during my lunch break from the hair salon. The air conditioning had been turned to MAX and I hurried to crank it back down. I wasn't made of money then and I'm sure as hell not now.

I froze in the doorway when I saw Doug in the bath. In my head, I was packing a bag and sprinting back to work, but I found myself kneeling down next to the tub. The blood was so dark that it was all I could take in at first. Then the slow drip of the faucet, matching every few beats of my thudding heart. I studied his pale face, the dull burst capillaries, his blond wispy hair. I imagined that he had left an explanation in a folded note on the sink: black ink on fancy cream-colored paper, like he'd really prepared for the moment.

I wanted the note to say:

Sorry for coming drunk to elementary school Father-Daughter Day.

Sorry for never buying you new clothes, Mirna Foul-smell.

Sorry for being such a fucking embarrassment.

But I probably wouldn't have gotten to read it anyway.

When he fluttered his eyelids, I yelped and pulled my hands to my chest. I couldn't stop the tears. I had nothing but anger left for this man and yet I'd lost control. I wept as he struggled to speak in a raspy voice so hoarse it sounded like he had been lost in the desert for days. But I didn't listen. I didn't want to hear any of it. Our father/daughter relationship had hit rock bottom and I wouldn't risk a whisper burying me deeper. All the good memories that I'd ever have were locked tight inside me. Nothing could change the addict before me, not even death. So when he mouthed, *I'm sorry*, I put two hands on his chest until he was under and all I could see were my arms disappearing into the murky red. Then I lost what little toughness I had left, along with my breakfast, on the floor. The wooden bat to the stomach when the bookie's men found me didn't help either. I guess in my shock I didn't hear them kick in the door. It's a shitty apartment and it came right off the hinges.

When I turned, too late to see the commotion, wiping the back of my sleeve over my mouth, the skinny one rammed me in the stomach like he was driving home a bayonet, expecting my guts to spill all over the floor. I'd seen people like him before, stalking the losers on the Strip. It was always the little guys with the baseball bat or flashlight, an extension of their dicks they could swing around in their hands. I doubled over, dry-heaving, my freshly manicured nails grasping for purchase on the linoleum. They laughed at the sight of Doug, like it was the funniest thing to hit Vegas in years. The Bat called him a bitch and said he took the easy way out. It hurt to agree. I knew Doug was broke. I'd paid the rent for the past two years. But I didn't know he was in deep with a bookie.

I stared up at the two men with blurred eyes bleeding mascara, recognizing that part of me knew this day would come. Doug had dragged me down into the gutter and now his dead body was chained to my ankle. I grew up around men who called themselves professional gamblers. I should have known. I'd seen Doug's friends fall to drugs and drink. Show up at the apartment with broken hands and busted faces. When it got bad, some cheated. And when it got worse, they turned to other sources of funds. Anything to get another shot at the money. Anything to feel another stack of chips.

The other thug I recognized. His fat head and braided goatee were unmistakable, even with the large 49ers cap pulled down low. My eyes must have given it away because he seemed startled all of a sudden and his face darkened. He worked security at Mermaid's, a dive casino located a few blocks off the strip where Doug had moved after he was no longer welcome at the major Vegas institutions. I'd been to Mermaid's a few times when Doug couldn't find his keys, let alone his feet.

The Bat grabbed a handful of my hair and yanked. The fuck already had my attention; now he was just playing with me. He gave me the short: Doug owed the bookie over one-hundred grand, and since I was family, I now owed the bookie over one-hundred grand. I'd challenge his bullshit definition of family and began to say something snippy to that effect, but he cut me off with the back of his hand. He told me I should be thankful he didn't use the bat.

While the Bat was giving his spiel, the Bouncer took to the rest of the apartment. I could hear drawers being emptied, the bed being tossed. The place wasn't big and he was through with it in under five. I got the sense he knew what he was looking for. The blood drained from my face when he returned with the thick roll of bills.

When I was sixteen, I caught Doug stealing from my ceramic piggy bank. He'd smashed it on the kitchen floor and was bent over, groping at the money. I moved to stop him and he struck me. It was a light, drunken punch, but it stung. I gathered two handfuls of cash and ran out the door. I wandered until my feet hurt and ended up outside of a Quick Cuts hair salon. I thought I saw one of Doug's gambling buddies so I ducked inside and sat down in the waiting area. It was cool, clean and smelled of cherry shampoo. I didn't realize I was still clutching the crumpled sweaty bills when the owner walked over to me.

She took pity; I could see it in her eyes. I wanted to run out the door but I was too hurt to be embarrassed. She coaxed me into a chair and gave me highlights and cut it into a short bob. She got me to open up. I told her about the gambling, Doug, the money. She listened without saying a word. When she spun me around in the chair and I saw my reflection, I could barely breathe. I felt alive. There was no way I could repay her, but I told her I'd help out after school. She eventually took me on as an assistant.

It wasn't much but I saved every dollar I could toward an education that would get me the hell away from Vegas.

It hurt more to see the cash in the Bouncer's hands than seeing Doug in the bath. Almost five grand for the Academy of Hair Design; I'd even sent in the application. He tossed the roll to the Bat who caught it and gave it a look like he'd rather light my dreams on fire to see me squirm than turn it over to his boss.

They dialed 911 for me and watched as I told the operator about Doug. The Bat cackled as they walked out with the money, issuing threats on my life and friends; they knew about the salon. When I watched the first cop who showed up outside the apartment complex fist-bump with the Bouncer, I knew I was in deep shit.

*****

I look out at the bright lights of the Vegas Strip through the large frosted window of the bathroom and I feel powerful, like I can take back this city and my life. I wonder if this feeling is what Doug was chasing after. I pull my dress on and stuff close to fifteen thousand in my purse. It's heavy, like the addiction I feel pumping in my veins. I walk out of the room like I've started my streak and I can see the Mustang down the hall. This is just the beginning.

Brass
by Roger Hobbs

It was a rainy Tuesday, around 7pm, when my boss dialed me up and told me he had a couple of big-balls hitmen coming to town. Since I was the low guy on the totem pole, it was my job to show them a good time. "Make sure you don't piss them off," he said. "These guys will waste a guy like you in a minute."

I started to say something, but my boss hung up on me before I could spit it out. I sighed, went to my bedstand, and wrote down the address where I was supposed to meet them. That was my job for the night, I guess. I was the babysitter to a couple of hitmen.

My name's Joe. In every criminal organization in the world, there's a guy like me. I'm the young guy in new leather who stands in the back keeping his mouth shut and his head down. The criminal world has a lot of room for advancement, sure, but just like any other job, it takes some time to get there. When you're as fresh to the game as I am, you're everybody's bitch. I bring coffee to wiseguys two times a day, and drive the working girls around so they don't miss a date. The first few years are just getting a foot in the door, I'm told, and right now that's where I am. Sure, I'm the lowest guy in a gang of low guys, but I can't complain. Before the Outfit I had to deal drugs and hold up gas stations just to survive, and I'd rather be somebody's bitch than spend one more minute selling black tar out in the freezing cold. When my boss calls me up and says I've got to show a couple of grade-A murdering buttonmen around for a night, I can't say no. It's just not how it works.

The address was this hotel bar way out by the Oregon Coast, maybe two hours away by car. I checked my watch. If I drove fast, I could probably beat the hitmen there and have time for a beer in the meanwhile. God knows I'd need one. I put on my leather jacket and was out the door in five minutes.

I'd never met these two hitmen coming in, but I'd heard about them. High-profile rub-outs don't happen much anymore, but when they have to, every organization has a couple of guys around to do the dirty work.

For the Outfit, our murderers were a pair of Italian brothers-in-law by the names of Vincent and Mancini. That's what everybody called them—Vincent and Mancini, like they were some sort of Abbott and Costello riff. I'd seen them once at an Outfit party, and heard stories through the ranks.

Vincent was the kind of guy who talked far more than he should have. He'd blab on and on, like he felt the need to narrate every single one of his daily experiences as they happened, all the time.

Mancini was the opposite, I'm told. He'd just sit there, listening to Vincent talk, and stare off into the distance, or sometimes right at the boss, like he was about to say something brilliant but he couldn't quite figure out how to put it. One never went anywhere without the other. If Vincent stood up to go to the bathroom, then Mancini would go too. It was like they were afraid to be alone, even just for a few seconds. They'd only split up if the job absolutely called for it.

They were an odd pair.

That Tuesday night the drive was easy. I got there in record time. The hotel bar was part of a little place out in

Seaside. The Outfit doesn't do much out in Seaside, but I knew my way around. It was a quiet little place with a long wild beach and Cape Cod-style architecture wind-bitten from the cold. A low fog rolled in off the Pacific Ocean and clung to the windows of the hotel bar like blood clots. Vincent and Mancini had beaten me there, I don't know how, and they looked up at me as I came through the door.

"Hey, fucker," Vincent said. "Are you the guy?"

"Yeah," I said. "I'm the guy."

"Then open a tab already."

And that was how we met. I laid my credit card down on the bar and ordered a double bourbon, neat.

When I first saw these guys a few months ago, Vincent and Mancini had been all expensive suits and ties. This night, though, they had switched back to what I could only presume was their usual attire: leather jackets, blue jeans and no-bull cigarettes. Mancini had perpetual stubble and hair as slick and black as a beaver pelt. There was a scar the size of a dollar bill along his cheek that turned pink when he drank. Vincent spoke to his brother in Italian and laughed loud enough to scare people. He was thinner and had cheekbones that sunk into his face like strip-mining pits.

I was ostensibly there to show them a good time, but I knew what was expected of me. Guys like these attracted trouble like flies to vinegar. Hitmen aren't like normal criminals. Normal criminals try to be subtle, but hitmen don't mind being noticed. They'd shoot a little girl in front of her parents, if they wanted to. I took the barstool next to them and Vincent clapped me on the back and tried to talk to me, but all I could think about was whether or not at the end of the night he was going to slit my throat and kill me. We fell into a conversation of sorts, but I can't remember half of it.

A lotta time passed that way.

I drank with Vincent and Mancini for hours. They ran up a six-hundred-dollar tab on my credit card, buying rounds for everybody in the place. Gran Patron. Johnnie Walker Blue. Grey Goose. Vincent's voice had a little squeak at the end of it, and when he drank it got louder and louder. The three of us moved to a back booth after a while, where nobody would bother us. After a few more rounds, Mancini took out a small mirror. He used the edge of a black American Express to cut cocaine into lines. Vincent and Mancini cut a whole bag into big, fat lines and did a couple though a five-hundred-Euro note. Mancini came up off his line with a look like molten lead on his face. It was something like pain, almost, but I couldn't tell. He was the kind of guy where you couldn't tell.

Vincent slapped him on the back and told him to do another.

I drank another bourbon and half-listened.

"Hey," Vincent said. "You smoke?"

I looked up from my drink. "What?"

"Come on," Vincent said. "Lets go outside and have a cig."

"Outside?"

"Yeah. Outside. Let's go."

Vincent basically picked me up by the collar. I got the impression I didn't have a choice in the matter, so I followed him out to the parking lot. Mancini followed me, flanking me between the two of them. It was half-raining, like it does by the coast, where the water pools up in the cracks in the pavement and sinks into the soft brown forest earth in great big sludge-like pools.

Vincent lit a Marlboro Red for himself and then another one for Mancini back behind the neon sign. The two just stared at me for a while, like I had just appeared out of the ether and they didn't know what to make of me. We stood like that for a while, in the rain, and listened to the sound of the ocean wind come through the pine trees and watched the rear floodlight flicker over the dumpsters.

Then, after a while, Vincent said, "You ever been in a fight, kid?"

I nodded, but didn't say anything.

Vincent smirked. He said, "Of course you haven't. Your hands are as soft as a baby's."

I said, "I got in a lot of fights when I was younger."

Vincent laughed and stared at me and took another deep drag off his Marlboro Red. He said, "That doesn't mean you've been in a fight. Not a real one. Maybe a few scuffles. Maybe some guy on your corner giving you lip, so you break his nose on a brick wall and put him down for a while. But I don't think you've ever really been in a fight. Not really. Not a drag out all-or-nothing brawl, the kind where you're spitting out teeth on the pavement and praying to God for it to just be over, before the adrenaline hits you full force and you let go with all your strength, pounding your fists into some guy and hoping that maybe one out of five makes contact because you know that when it does, you're going to straight up kill that motherfucker."

I said, "I don't like fighting."

"Nobody does," he said. "Not if you do it right."

Vincent took another drag off the cigarette and I got a good look at his hands. His knuckles looked like a construction site, with deep brown scarred ridges and heavy bulging calluses at the top of his fingers. He held his cigarette like another man might hold a pencil. There was no finesse in his hands. His thumbs were the size of sausages.

Mancini flicked the butt of the cigarette and took a set of gold-plated brass knuckles from his left jacket pocket. There were scratches along the ridges where the gold plating had flaked away to reveal the solid steel underneath. He slipped them over the glove on his right hand and flexed his fingers until they were snug right above his second knuckles. He formed a fist. The metal caught the light and glimmered. Mancini didn't say anything. He took a small vial of cocaine out of his pocket, poured a little on the soft spot between his first finger and this thumb, and snorted it.

Vincent said, "You ever been punched with brass knuckles, kid?"

I didn't say anything.

Vincent said, "It's much more important to know how to avoid getting hit. You see, the knuckles preserve the force of the punch by concentrating it all into one small little place on the hand. Makes the punch stronger, and keeps you from breaking your fingers when you give it. Normally if you want to kill a guy with a punch, you've got to practically break your hand to do it. This makes things easier."

"Kill?"

"Yeah, you heard me. Kill. A sap or a stun gun knocks a guy out. Brass knuckles don't. They break bones. Powder teeth. Snap ribs like a twig. You don't punch a guy with brass knuckles to incapacitate him. You punch a guy with brass knuckles if you want to crack open his skull and send fragments of his nose into his brain. You punch a guy with brass knuckles if you want to break a man's jaw so hard he bites off his tongue and swallows it."

I didn't say anything. Mancini stood there in the half-light, looking up at the flickering neon sign. He didn't move. He hardly even breathed.

Vincent said, "Mancini here? He got hit by brass knuckles. We were just kids, you know. Seventeen, maybe eighteen. It was a fight outside church one Sunday afternoon. This dealer came up from the left while we were walking out of service and blindsided Mancini with a right hook, knuckledusters to the jaw. Mancini went down after that. Lost about ten teeth, bits of his gums, a good half his tongue. He spat it out on the pavement like chewing gum. Had a hole in his cheek he could breathe through. But Mancini got up. Kicked the guy in the kneecap to bring him down. Beat that kid to death, right there on the church steps. Took him by the collar and slammed his head into the marble until his skull broke and his eyes went dark."

Mancini didn't say anything.

Vincent said, "Ever since then, he's kind of had a thing for brass knuckles. Every guy's got a preference, and that's his. Some go for knives, some for shotguns, some for piano wire. But Mancini? Brass knuckles."

I said, "What's your point?"

"What's my point? Look around you. If you want to survive in this business, you have to know what you're dealing with."

I shook my head.

Vincent said, "My point is, if you're going to work with men like us, you've got to know what it's like to kill someone up close. Personal. As far away as you're standing from me, right now, no further. If you're going to work with us, you've got to kill someone close enough to smell their fear and watch their eyes go dark. Plunge a Ka-Bar into somebody's chest until you can feel his heart stop. Can you do that?"

I said, "I told you, I don't like fighting."

He said, "And killing?"

I shook my head. "That especially."

"That's cute," Vincent said. "Real cute. You practice that? You say that to yourself in front of the mirror?"

"It's true."

"Well, I hope you've got it in you. Because if the moment comes, you better have the stuff to finish the job. Because if you're holding us up, I won't hesitate to put you down."

"You won't--"

And just like that, Mancini took a swing at me.

It was a big and wide and dirty thing, one of those punches that people don't get up after. He punched with the force of his whole body behind it. Stepped forward, wound up, and everything. If the punch had made contact, it would have left me in a puddle of blood and spinal fluid right there in the parking lot. It didn't, though. The shot was wide and I jerked to the left on pure reflex. Mancini stumbled after the miss.

I grabbed his hand by the brass knuckles and twisted his wrist back. The joint came to a lock and his arm straightened out against the unnatural motion. From there I twisted clockwise. The wrist doesn't naturally allow much rotational motion, so all of the ligaments locked up. There are a bunch of nerve endings at the base of the bones in the forearm, near the bottom of the wrist. I kept going until his bones were pressing right into them.

Mancini screamed.

I took a quick step behind him and twisted his whole arm around with me. He stumbled with me because of the pain. I twisted his arm back until it was completely straight, then pushed my other hand into the small of his back. Now all of his joints locked up, from the shoulder to elbow. Three times the pain. I held him like that for a second to make sure he could feel the full extent of the agony. If I wanted, a small punch would shatter all the bones in his arm.

Vincent drew a gun.

It was a small thing, a Beretta Tomcat with that matte-black finish that blended into the shadows. He held it sideways in one hand and took a bead at my head. I pulled up Mancini by the collar and put him between me and Vincent as a human shield. Mancini was like butter in my hands now. The pain made him compliant.

We froze like that for a moment. Cars rushed by on the highway in the distance and wind blew off the ocean through the pine trees. The neon bar sign flickered and then went out. I jostled Mancini again, twisting his elbow joint against his veins and cutting off circulation to his arm. He clenched his jaw and the scar on his face turned purple.

Vincent smiled. Started to laugh. The sound came up from deep in his diaphragm, like I'd just told the greatest joke in history. He put down the gun and slid it back into his pocket. He raised his other hand up with an open palm to show he meant no harm.

I released Mancini. He stumbled away from me like a drunk and fell to his knees, clasping his arm in his hands. Just like that, as suddenly as the fighting started, it stopped. We were friends again. Comrades. Partners in crime.

Vincent said, "I'm sorry about that. We had to make sure you were cool."

"So you tried to smash my face in? What would you have done if you succeeded?"

"Buried you. Out by the coast, probably. I hear bodies wash up there all the time. But it didn't happen. You're good."

I didn't say anything. The door to the bar opened and a group of people came out. They looked at us as they went to their van. Mancini was still on the ground, breathing slow.

Vincent turned to him. Said, "It still hurts?"

Mancini nodded. Didn't say anything.

"Did you really swing at him with all you got?"

Mancini was quiet for a moment. He grabbed his elbow and kept his arm straight as he worked himself up off his knees. When he spoke his voice was slurred and broken, like his mouth was full of cotton balls. When he opened his mouth I could see the rough stub of his tongue, and the scars on the inside of his cheeks.

He said, "Kid's alright."

Vincent came over and patted me on the back. He pushed a cigarette out of his pack for me. I took it, just so I wouldn't have to explain to him that I didn't smoke. I held it in my hand until Vincent was done smoking his, then discretely dropped it on the sidewalk. We walked back to the car in silence. I sat in the back seat and watched the cones of our headlights pierce through the forest.

From that moment on, Vincent and Mancini treated me like I was one of them. A brother. They told me all their dirty jokes and stood up for me whenever they thought I was being threatened. They invited me to eat with them and they ordered me a drink whenever they were having one. I wasn't sure how I felt about that. Vincent and Mancini were ready to die for one another, and they'd both die for me.

"You've got brass ones, kid," Vincent said. "Like one of us."

Under The Bus
By Albert Tucher

"Check this out," said Mary Alice.

She slid her smart phone across the table. Diana moved her Greek salad and diet soda aside and centered the phone in front of her.

"Now there's something you don't see every day," she said. "A naked man with a hard-on."

"Comedian," said Mary Alice. "You've already seen it twice before lunch. So have I, but never mind that. Look at his face."

"What about it?"

"That's the face of family values."

"No wonder I don't know him."

"Len Howard? Mister Social Conservative of Warren County? He's the one who started the crackdown out there."

"The one who's yelling about prostitution in his fair city?"

"That's him."

"I figured he was worried about his reelection and just looking for an issue."

"He is. But take a wild guess how he knows about it."

"He's a client. Surprise, surprise."

"If he hasn't gotten to you, he will. I think he's pretty new at this hobby of his."

Diana knew how that went—a man found out that he could buy hot and cold running sex, and he went crazy.

For some men it was just a phase, but others never got over it.

"How did you get him to hold still for the picture?"

Mary Alice grinned. "I told him to close his eyes and he'd get something special."

Diana took another look. Howard's eyes were indeed closed in the picture.

"Did he? Get something special, I mean."

"Of course. I run an honest business here. But now I have some insurance if he ever tries to throw me under the bus."

Diana didn't comment, but Mary Alice's plan was a bad idea. If it really came down to it, a hooker was better off taking her lumps than threatening an influential man.

"Matter of fact," said Mary Alice, "I think I'll email this to the group, so everybody will know what's going on."

That was an even worse idea. Diana and Mary Alice both belonged to an online discussion group, where women in the business vented and shared information about good clients, bad clients, reliable gynecologists, and police crackdowns. New members had to come with an introduction from a veteran, and years earlier Diana had sponsored Mary Alice.

But everything runs its course after a while.

"I've been getting a bad feeling about that group," said Diana. "I think some of the new girls aren't girls at all. I think they're clients, or maybe law enforcement."

"Like who?"

"Jacki, for instance. Ever notice how she's always asking questions, but she never contributes anything?"

"I know her. Matter of fact, I'm her sponsor. You're just paranoid."

"That's healthy in this business."

"Well, until she actually does something… Anyway, here goes."

"I wouldn't," said Diana.

Mary Alice's finger hovered over the touch screen, until she dropped her hand into her lap.

"You always spoil the fun," she said.

"You mean you know I'm right."

"Whatever."

Mary Alice picked the phone up and put it back in her bag.

That was Monday. On Thursday Diana had no clients to see until the afternoon. She decided to let the rush hour traffic peter out before heading to Fanelli's gym for a workout. A little after nine she made sure her gym bag had the necessities and headed for the front door.

As she reached for the knob, the doorbell rang. That stopped her. She wasn't expecting anyone, and she didn't like surprises.

The spyhole showed her a reason for concern—three strange men who had found their way to her front steps. She took another look and pegged them. They weren't holding *Watchtower* magazines or anything similar, but they still glowed with the clean-cut, barely contained aggression of proselytizers. Diana opened the inner door and spoke through the screen.

"Sorry, gentlemen. I'm not what you're looking for."

"Actually, you are," said the forty-ish man in the center of the group. He was the only one in a suit and tie, and his body language said he was in charge. "You're Diana Andrews."

The other two were husky twenty-somethings in polo shirts and khakis. They looked like brothers, maybe even twins, with their blond buzz cuts and their arms folded in identical macho-man poses. She was supposed to be intimidated.

"We would like to speak with you inside," said the older man.

Diana pushed the screen door open so it bounced off the nearer of the two young men. Without thinking he took a step back and flailed with his arms as his foot found nothing but air. He caught himself two steps down. His face turned red with anger.

She closed the screen door again and latched it.

"I don't know you."

The older man gave her a glare, but she had seen better ones.

"Okay," he said. "We represent Mr. Len Howard."

"I don't know him, either."

"That's what we would like to talk to you about."

She kept looking at him and waiting for him to remember his manners.

"And my name is Paul Porterfield."

Diana still didn't like this situation, but she had to find out what Porterfield wanted. A man who knew both her business and her home address had her at a disadvantage.

"Please come in."

The young men started to follow him, but she froze them with a look.

"One strange man at a time, please."

Porterfield nodded at his companions, who scowled but stayed put on the steps. Diana led him down the short hall and to the right, into her living room. She pointed toward her aging sofa and took her single armchair. She didn't get much company.

"What's with the bodyguards?"

"Mr. Howard gets threats. Righteous men always do."

"So why aren't they with him now? Let me guess. He gave them the slip. Sometimes he does that, and you just found out what he does while he's off the leash. Am I right?"

"I thought you didn't know him."

"I don't. I know of him."

"Len Howard has a great future ahead of him. He could be governor. New Jersey desperately needs to restore God to His rightful place."

"Seems to me God could have chosen better."

"All men are frail. I wish Len had picked another brand of weakness, but there it is." He looked at her. "Maybe you can explain it to me. Why do so many men choose to self-destruct in this particular way?"

"I can think of worse things he could do. He's not molesting children, is he?"

Porterfield closed his eyes for a moment as if saying a prayer of thanks.

"I have an arrangement to offer you. Mr. Howard will do what he will do, and it might as well be with you. You have a good reputation by the standards of your business."

"Thanks, I think."

"He will pay you your going rate, of course. Then I will pay you the same again to keep me informed."

"No."

"No?"

He made it sound like a language that he didn't speak.

"I thought you were in business for the money."

"That's why I'm saying no, because it would kill my business. You said I have a good reputation. In this business you get a good rep by keeping your mouth shut about clients. Period."

He studied her and saw nothing to encourage him. He got up.

"If you won't help us, I suggest that you stay in Sussex County. Warren is about to get too hot for you."

"I don't like threats. Jacki."

"What?"

"That's you, isn't it? Online, I mean."

"No."

She studied him. He had the smug look of a man who thought he could fool her by telling the literal truth. He knew who Jacki was.

"Never mind," she said.

Porterfield stood and started for the door without another word to her. She could live with that. When she heard the front door open and shut, she went to the spyhole and verified that he and his muscle men had left.

She went back to plan A. As she started the drive to Fanelli's gym, she got an annoying surprise. Her power lock had stopped working on the driver's side, which would mean a brief but expensive visit to the mechanic.

It could wait.

All through her step class and upper body workout, Diana thought about Paul Porterfield. As she drove home again, she decided to tell the online group about the encounter. He might try someone else.

Her computer was on her grandmother's old oak desk in the spare room of her rented Cape Cod. Diana logged into the group. Before she could compose her post, she noticed that Jacki had resurfaced with a message of her own just six minutes earlier, asking if anyone wanted a new client in the Driscoll area. Jacki didn't want him, because he wanted Greek.

That happened. Women in the business offered to trade a client for a favor down the line. But Diana had met several men who tried to talk her into anal sex by saying they could get it from Jacki.

Maybe Jacki was tired of walking funny and figured that she had enough business to do without it, or maybe online Jacki wasn't the real Jacki.

Diana went to the phone on her kitchen wall and speed-dialed Mary Alice.

"I need to know. Who's Jacki?"

"Why?"

"She's giving me an itch. I think the group is compromised, and that could be very bad. For us, clients, everybody."

"I still think you're paranoid, but okay. Jacki Greenwald. I met her the way you met me. Remember?"

Issue Four

Diana did remember Mary Alice accosting her years earlier in the parking lot of the Savoy motel. Newly divorced, Mary Alice had been sleeping around and thinking about getting paid for it.

"So you got her started with some referrals?"

"For a cut of the first date with each one. You know the drill."

"Have you seen her lately?"

"No," said Mary Alice after a pause. "Now that you mention it. We used to have lunch once in a while, but she canceled the last couple of times."

Diana went back to the computer and sent Jacki an email off-group. She couldn't post an accusation until she was sure.

Jacki's reply arrived ten minutes later. "Send me your contact info. I'll have him get in touch with you."

"I want some face time with you first," Diana typed. "I don't do referrals with anyone I haven't met."

"Lunch tomorrow?"

Diana sat back in surprise. She had expected Jacki to make an excuse, which would have confirmed her suspicions.

"It'll have to be Mickey D's by the no-name motel off I-80," Jacki wrote. "I have dates there. Two o'clock?"

"Works for me."

The location was a nice touch. So was the time. A lot of clients got away from the office for lunchtime dates, which left hookers getting a bite where and when they could. This time Diana didn't believe it, though.

At two sharp she sat at a booth with coffee in front of her. She never ate McDonald's. Jacki didn't keep her waiting. Diana liked the woman's look, with her petite figure, enormous brown eyes and mass of curly dark hair. Jackie had a Happy Meal and a diet Sprite on her tray.

"Not eating?" said Jacki.

"I had something earlier."

"So, what can I tell you?" Jacki smiled. "I'd want to meet you if the roles were reversed."

"You know Mary Alice."

"She's great. Very generous. And gorgeous. That dark and dangerous look is my type. I understand you were her, uh, mentor."

"Interesting way to put it."

Diana's curt reply and unwavering scrutiny made Jacki start to squirm.

"You're interested in this client?"

"Maybe."

"I mean, that's why you're here, right?"

Diana kept looking at the other woman.

"Well, he's here. I canceled on him, but he says he never got the email. You can go right over."

"That's convenient."

"Well, sometimes things work out that way."

"Not this time."

Diana slid out of the booth and got up to go. Jacki's mouth hung open unattractively.

"You know what else is convenient?"

Diana stared down at the other woman.

"This location, that's what. Most people wouldn't know, but I pay attention to things like jurisdiction. I'm surprised you even tried this on me. That motel is about six feet into Len Howard territory."

She left her untouched coffee for Jacki to deal with and headed for the exit.

Outside Diana scanned the area. She didn't see what she was looking for, until she went around the building to the overflow parking lot in the rear. She knew an unmarked car when she saw one, and the old acquaintance behind the wheel of this dark blue Taurus confirmed it. He gave her a sheepish grin.

"Hey, Diana."

"McGarrity, what's up?"

"Wasting time, that's what. Comes with the job."

"I assume you were listening."

"Yeah, she's wired. Orders from on high."

"Relax, I didn't think this was your idea."

"Like we don't have better things to worry about. You don't make us look bad, so we don't bother you. Everybody's happy except the brass."

"I doubt the brass like pressure from politicos."

"You're probably right."

"And to think I could have made myself bulletproof."

"How?"

"By taking Len Howard on as a client. His right-hand man came to me about it."

"He'd throw you under the bus in a second."

"I know. That was irony. What's your hold on Jacki? Does she get to stay out of jail?"

"She's cooperating voluntarily," said McGarrity. "Seems she's born again."

"Maybe I should go back and tell her about Howard's hobby."

"Hell, she knows. She says human nature is frail."

"You know, I like that. If I ever get busted, I'll plead human frailty."

"It only works for guys. Even then it's just the ones with juice."

"Don't I know it."

The whole business should have been history, but it didn't feel like history. She couldn't figure out why, until she got a page from an unfamiliar number.

Most women in the business had gone to cell phones for business, but Diana planned to stick with the old pager and pay phone system for as long as she could. She found it more secure. She dropped coins and punched buttons.

"My name is Len Howard," said a male voice.

"Oh. Mr. Howard."

With most new clients it took some effort to pry a name out of them. Mary Alice must be right about

Howard. He was in the giddy, reckless stage of this new hobby. He might be seeing two or three women a day.

The negotiations took hardly any time.

"Gifts in the two-hundred-dollar range are appreciated," she told him.

"That's fine. The Savoy Motel?"

That surprised her for a moment, but it shouldn't have.

"You understand," he said, "Current political factors make it necessary for me to stay out of Warren County for matters like this. Don't soil the nest, you know what I mean."

"Of course."

"I hope you know that this situation won't last. It's an unfortunate necessity."

Fucking us and then arresting us, Diana could have said but didn't. *Unfortunate, yes. Necessity, I don't know.*

"Whatever you need to do," was what she did say.

As long as that included paying her.

The Savoy was five minutes away. She seldom used it anymore, and mostly for a few clients who dated back to her earliest days, when she hadn't known enough to maintain a bigger privacy zone. But the client's money talked, and if it said the Savoy, the Savoy it was.

She arrived two minutes early and got out of the car. Before locking the door and committing herself, she looked around. She didn't like what she saw.

The problem was a dark Lexus sitting in the far corner of the lot. Most men who bought sex parked as close as they could to the sanctuary of the motel room or office. The windows of the Lexus were also fogged, as if someone was still in it.

There was a first time for everything, but she had never seen the cops use a car like that on stakeout. Somehow that didn't make her feel better, and she decided to listen to her instincts.

She got back into her Taurus and thrust the key into the ignition. She started the engine and tried to back up. The tires of the Lexus screeched as the luxury car accelerated into her path. Three doors flew open. Porterfield's two young thugs lurched out onto the blacktop. The two young men ran toward her, as she put the transmission in drive and wrenched the wheel. If she could make her turn circle tight enough, she could get to the exit before they got to her.

She missed, and had to stop and try to reverse. The transmission stuck for a moment in neutral. In that moment one of the young men yanked her driver's door open and grabbed her bicep. He had a painful grip.

That's what I get, she thought.

She should have gone to the mechanic right away. Reaching for the manual door lock had been one thing too many while she was doing everything at once.

Porterfield climbed out of the Lexus and strolled up to her with that insufferable look on his face.

"We're going to take a ride."

"Mr. Howard is waiting for me."

"Let him. He's already seen two of your colleagues today."

The young man pulled her out of her seat. He and his twin marched her to the Lexus and pushed her into the back seat. The same young man joined her in the back and this time clutched her right arm. He seemed to enjoy inflicting pain, which didn't surprise her.

The other young man drove. Should she learn their names? She was seeing a lot of them. Porterfield turned his body in the passenger seat to look at her.

"I need you to do something for me."

She ignored him. She would find out soon enough what he wanted, and right now she felt like annoying him. He turned away.

They drove south on Route 15 and picked up I-80 west. That told her what she needed to know. Three exits later they left the interstate and pulled into the parking lot of the no-name motel.

The three men climbed out. Diana didn't feel like cooperating, but the driver came back to open her door and pull her from the seat. Again the two bodyguards pinned her between them. They walked her toward a room around the side of the square building. Porterfield took a key card from his suit coat pocket. He inserted it in a room marked 117.

"In," he told her.

He turned to the two young men. "Wait outside."

Inside the room the lights were on. She could hardly miss Jacki lying on the floor.

Diana had seen death a number of times, and as always, there was no mistaking it. Jacki lay on her back. She had surrendered unconditionally to gravity, and her head tilted so sharply to her left that her temple rubbed her shoulder. Only a broken neck would permit such an angle.

Diana pulled her eyes away and focused on Porterfield.

"Why?" she said. "Why would he kill her?"

Porterfield's lack of expression told her everything.

"He didn't. Howard didn't kill her. You did. Do your sidekicks know that? I'll bet they don't. They'd accept it from Howard, but not from you."

Still no reaction from him.

"You pathetic piece of shit. You wanted some of your boss's scraps, and she wouldn't put out. Right?"

"I didn't kill her," said Porterfield. "You did."

"I figured that was what this is about."

"You confronted her about trying that sting on you. And you argued, and you broke her neck."

"I'm in shape, but I'm not that strong."

"You were in a rage. You didn't know your own strength."

She decided it wasn't worth arguing. Porterfield took her silence for surrender.

"Now you're going to call 911 and confess. I know cops. They love a confession, and they'll love taking two of you off the board at once."

"Why would I confess?"

"To stay alive. If you don't you'll disappear. People like you disappear all the time."

"And if I do?"

"You'll do a few years for manslaughter. Free room and board. Then you get out and get on with your pathetic life. There will be some money for you in it."

"Money," said Diana. "Now you're speaking my language."

Porterfield hadn't expected that. He studied her.

"Be very sure about this. Don't think you can put anything over on me. If I get that idea, I'll get rid of you and take my chances."

"You don't give me much choice."

That seemed to satisfy him. He took out a cell phone and handed it to her.

"It's prepaid," he said. "It can't be traced to me. And it's expired, so don't bother trying to call anyone but 911."

"You've thought of everything."

"That's what I do for a living."

Diana took the phone and made the call. She explained where she was to the operator.

"Somebody's dead here. It just happened."

The operator sounded as if she heard it all the time. "Stay on the line. The officers will be right there."

Porterfield stared at her for another long moment. When he was satisfied, he opened the door and closed it behind him. Through the door she heard the faint sound of an upscale engine starting and then accelerating smoothly. It faded, but she knew the Lexus would stay close by.

The operator asked one innocuous question, and then another. It was obvious what she was trying to do.

"Relax," said Diana. "I'm not going anywhere."

Five minutes later came a knock, the kind that only cops knew how to do.

"They're here," Diana told the operator.

She ended the call and set the phone down on the cheap table in the corner. She opened the door. It was just one young man in uniform. She didn't know him. He looked so young that she was afraid she had been hooking longer than he had been breathing.

Diana nodded toward Jacki's body on the floor. The young cop motioned to her to turn around and raise her arms. He frisked her and then cuffed her wrists behind her. It was her second experience of handcuffs, and the experience hadn't improved.

He pointed to the flimsy chair by the cheap circular table in the corner of the room. She went and sat. With her hands and arms trapped between her own back and the hard back of the chair, she hoped she wouldn't have to stay there long.

She didn't speak. Neither did the officer. About fifteen very long minutes later another knock sounded. The uniformed officer opened the door and admitted the detective Diana had been hoping for. That was the good thing about small police departments.

"Hey, Diana."

"McGarrity, what's up?"

He nodded at the uniformed officer, who went outside and closed the door behind him. McGarrity looked at Jacki on the floor and then back at Diana.

"Switchboard says you confessed."

"Not exactly."

He looked around some more. He was slow and methodical about it.

"So," he said. "What are those assholes trying to pull?"

She explained.

"Could be hard to prove if the bodyguards back him up," said McGarrity.

"They will. You have a smartphone?"

"A dinosaur like me? Come on."

"I don't either. Your uniform looks young enough to be digital."

McGarrity went to the door and opened it. He spoke to the uniformed officer, who came back inside. McGarrity nodded, and the young man unlocked the handcuffs. Diana refused to rub her wrists in front of the two cops, but the relief was sweet.

"Give her your phone for a minute."

The young cop was careful to keep his face expressionless, but disapproval came through in his movements. He held his cell phone out at arm's length. Diana took it and thumbed in numbers that she knew well. She was afraid the call would go to voicemail, but Mary Alice answered.

"You still have that picture of Len Howard? Email it to this number, okay?"

"What happened to taking your lumps?"

"That was when we were talking about a hooker bust. This is a lot more than that."

"Okay, but I'm earning some 'I told you so' points here."

"No argument from me."

The photo arrived seconds later. Diana held the phone out to McGarrity.

"Please," he said. "I just ate."

"Try being me for a day."

"How am I supposed to use this?"

"You can lie to a suspect, can't you?"

"Howard's not a suspect."

"Make him think he is. Make him think Jacki took the picture. Then give him a chance to throw Porterfield under the bus. When he does that, the two sidekicks will give him up. They know he was here."

He nodded.

"I've made it work with less than that. No guarantees, though."

"Kind of like life."

Gallows Point
by Sam Wiebe

Mid-afternoon and the sky was a wreath of smoke over the ash-gray water. The Bastard would be on the afternoon ferry from Departure Bay. His first time on the mainland since retirement.

From the terminal parking lot the Old Man watched the fat white boat cut a stately pace through the gray waves. Ten minutes. Rain swept over the windshield in streaks. The Old Man rotated the ignition key enough to make the wiper blades fling the water to the margins of the pane. The Bastard was long-legged and extremely tall. Remembering this, the Old Man bent and adjusted the passenger's seat back. Then he opened the glovebox and transferred the pistol to the stash below the armrest.

The boat docked. The ramp came down. The foot passengers left the vehicle deck. The Bastard was last off the boat, trailing behind two crew members. His clothes were outdated. Old age had stooped him, undercutting his height. The Old Man flipped on the headlights. The Bastard veered toward them without seeming to change direction. The Bastard's paleness and height made his movements seem uncanny, almost spectral.

When both of them were in the car they shook hands.

"Hope the ferry ride was tolerable," the Old Man began.

"Infrequency makes it so. And yourself?"

"Alive. Healthy."

"And therein lies the problem."

Even with the seat reclined, the Bastard's knees grazed the underside of the dash. The Old Man had turned slightly to face him. The Bastard stared straight ahead, smiling. His smile coaxed unpleasant memories from the Old Man.

"Retirement doesn't agree with everyone," the Bastard said. "Your responsibilities dwindle. You linger over past mistakes. I assume your invitation sprang from sheer boredom."

"We have unfinished business," the Old Man said.

"You might. Myself, I'm living a fulfilling retirement."

"But you're here."

"Only to prevent you coming to me. But yes. I'm here. Speak."

"I've had health problems," the Old Man said. "I come through 'em all right, but I got to thinking about regrets. 'Member the last time we saw each other?"

"That would be Bonn," the Bastard said. "Shortly before the Amnesty."

The Old Man nodded. "I saw you come out of a picture show. You'd gotten Higgs and Mulcahy the day before. And Chen, I think, though we didn't find her till after."

"I remember Chen," the Bastard said fondly. "Now that was a job."

"I followed you three blocks, arguing with myself, whether or not to kill you."

"And?"

"I made the wrong choice."

"Since we're both still here," the Bastard said, "I'd respectfully disagree. And perhaps remind you that it was your side that declared Amnesty and forced retirement on us all. One can't break rules to uphold rules."

"I don't know that the rules apply to you."

"Do you have a gun within reach?"

The Old Man nodded. The Bastard smiled.

"I've never found much use for them."

"Too fast for you, I expect. Over too soon."

"Hardly," the Bastard said. "I consider firearms a tool of domination. They're most effective, as you know, in situations that don't absolutely necessitate their use. Cowards oppressing cowards. The righteous tool is the one that consumes both wielder and adversary, making each encounter a battle of destinies."

"Tell all that to Chen."

"I did," the Bastard said. "Showed her the detonator and she surrendered herself to me."

"And you took her apart. 'Long with three or four civilians."

"Weapons of absolute liberty are indiscriminate."

The Old Man thought about this. "You're wired now?"

"Of course. Always."

"Since retirement? Even in your home?"

"It's only paranoia if you can guarantee no one's coming for you. If people will hold to the rules of retirement without exception. Your call disproves that."

The ferry was now taking in cars for its return trip. The parking lot had been emptied save for the Old Man's rental and two others. A line of cabs waited by the terminal entrance, the drivers gossiping under the awning.

"As I see it," the Bastard said quietly, "it comes down to whether your late-blooming sense of justice equals my need for unqualified, unhindered freedom. Whether you wish to make that trade."

The Old Man lifted the armrest and produced the gun. Carefully he placed it on the dashboard. They stared at it. The killing machine's barrel stared back at them with the simple blunt defiance of an unadorned fact.

The Bastard nodded. He didn't gloat. "I believe I'll catch that return ferry."

The Old Man's hand wavered over the lock mechanism. "What if I told you I accept that trade?"

"I don't know I'd believe you," the Bastard said.

"Then hit the damn detonator."

The foghorn of another inbound vessel sounded.

"Seems a shabby end for two professionals," the Bastard said.

"One professional. One war criminal."

"As you fancy. How about something more sporting?"

"You're talking a fair fight?" The Old Man listened attentively.

"I saw a film once," the Bastard said. "Two great swordsmen agree to duel to the death. They set a year for preparations. They choose a remote island. One year to the day, they row to the beach and do battle, steel on steel. I won't ruin the conclusion."

"I can guess," the Old Man said. "Name the island."

"There are two in Nanaimo Harbor. Protection Island is residential. Newcastle is a public reserve."

"So Newcastle."

"Protection. After dark. At an aptly-named landmark called Gallows Point."

"Civilians--"

"We'll be discreet."

The Old Man thought it over and nodded.

"One year from today then," the Bastard said. "It's something to look forward to." Smiling. "Now. Shall we flip a coin to decide who steps out of the car first?"

*****

It was possible of course that the Bastard meant to murder him prior to their rendezvous. The Old Man found it good practice to live as if that was likely. He'd always lived aware of others, of the slightest variation in mood or noise. Now he once again had reason to.

He learned about Protection Island. The history of the coal mines that ran underneath Nanaimo Harbor. The explosion that had killed a hundred whites and fifty-three

Chinese. Protection Island's rebirth as homes for the wealthy. He studied nearby Newcastle Island too, since at low tide one could wade between them. A rare species of albino raccoon prowled its shores. A Hawaiian convict lay buried on Newcastle in an unmarked location. The Old Man studied them but he didn't visit them. That would somehow violate the pact he and the Bastard had made. He'd have to cede to the Bastard the advantage of terrain.

He picked his tools and his attire carefully. He knew the Bastard might use explosives. The Bastard favored cheap radio detonators and the most rudimentary land mines. That was another advantage the Old Man would yield. He would never employ explosives again.

He decided on an air taxi to take him across the Georgia Straight to Nanaimo, and then a rented boat with a thick plastic windshield and a powerful outboard motor. He wanted to limit his exposure on the water. The Bastard might decide that the contest began when the first one of them reached Gallows Point. And the Old Man knew the Bastard would be there first.

He considered his own advantages but took no comfort in them.

*****

In the air the Old Man settled his stomach and said his goodbyes to the city. He was anxious. How could he not be? He had done nothing like this—nothing at all, really—for years.

He held two fingers to his neck and listened to the thrum of the plastic replacement heart in his chest. His pulse was elevated but steady. He thought of Chen, of Higgs and Mulcahy. He wondered what they would've been like at his age. Would they have taken to retirement? Higgs, maybe. Not the others.

He'd outfitted himself in dark clothing and carried his gear in a red nylon hockey bag. He'd tinted his hair dark so that no one would try to assist him with his luggage out of sympathy. He'd avoid people, but more importantly they'd avoid him.

In a Nanaimo diner he put away acidic coffee and stared at grub he didn't want. He reminded himself he was doing this for justice. Not selfish reasons like revenge. Least of all out of idleness, the "sheer boredom" the Bastard had spoken of. He'd settle things with the Bastard, get justice, or go down swinging, the way the others had.

At dusk he walked to the marina and paid a man in cash for the use of the boat. The Old Man checked it thoroughly. He inspected the motor and made sure there were no superfluous wires. Satisfied, he paid the dealer. The dealer told him to be careful, boating at night.

Protection Island wasn't five miles from shore. Houses and moored yachts gleamed in the fading light. Newcastle lay to the north, thick deciduous forest set back from peach-colored sand.

His new vessel was called the *Bran Mak Morn*. The name meant nothing to him.

Halfway across the bay he realized he had to piss. He could see no one on the docks, nothing glinting from the yachts save the odd bit of brass or chrome trim. He eased off the throttle until the boat was coasting and did his business off the port side, feeling exposed. The city glow from the harbor was slight. It wasn't tourist season.

The sun fell. There was a light rain. He slipped a paddle into the water, preferring not to use the motor for the last part. He knew the Bastard was watching him. Probably had been since he cast off from the marina. But from where, was the question. If it was him...

The Old Man considered it. The best vantage would be one of the houses, or the trees behind them. The yachts would offer an advantage of proximity and escape. But he wasn't sure the Bastard would employ the water. The stooped way he'd moved back on the mainland...

Issue Four

The Old Man chastised himself. He was falling into familiar patterns of thought, patterns that hadn't helped him back before retirement. You couldn't anticipate the Bastard. You couldn't outthink him. The Old Man would have to trust his instincts, and treat Protection Island as if every square foot could be weaponized.

He clambered out of the boat onto the jetty. He'd bent to retrieve the bag when a bullet punched through the windshield close to his cheek.

Off-kilter, he tipped clumsily back into the boat and flattened himself. His hearing was still keen, but he hadn't heard the shot.

Lying staring up at the stars he put the trajectory together. It had come from Newcastle Island. A precision shot, more than half a mile. He hadn't expected the Bastard to use a rifle.

He turned onto his belly, spun around and peered up through the screen. He could see nothing on the other island save the outline of trees. The adrenaline chill was a comfort.

He set to work. First he slipped down into the seat and brought the engine to life. Keeping his head low, he corrected the course so the boat would graze the western point of Newcastle Island. It might run aground. It didn't matter either way.

A nylon cord would keep the wheel from correcting. He eased up the throttle and secured that, then flicked on the pair of powerful lamps built into the prow of the boat.

He heard the crack of the second shot, and the third, both aimed at the neon lamps that lit up the beach on Newcastle. The Old Man slung the bag over his arm. He killed the lamps and in the sudden darkness dropped into the water.

The water was cold and he couldn't quite touch bottom. It took effort to pull the floating bag underwater. He couldn't have it bobbing above the waves as he swam.

He'd scouted Newcastle well and knew that the rocky eastern beach offered the best cover and the shortest stretch of exposed ground to the trees. Northeast, the sandbars rose and it was there you could walk between islands at low tide. The Bastard might wait for him there. He might already be waiting at the eastern beach. In the past the Old Man had often felt that the Bastard had access to his thought processes. He wondered what preparations the Bastard had made. Perhaps none. Maybe that morning the Bastard had simply taken down the rifle, stuffed his pockets with cartridges, and set out to ambush the Old Man. There was no accounting for the Bastard.

Water crept into his nostrils. He swam awkwardly, the bag upending him, careful his strokes didn't break the water's surface. He paused to take in air and check that the *Bran Mak Morn* was still on target. It seemed to be slowing. He reached the rocky isthmus and felt his waterlogged shoes touch the island. Above the lap of the waves he could hear little. He pulled himself up, remaining behind the barnacle-flecked rocks. He'd imprinted a map of Newcastle in his mind. He knew the distance he'd have to cross to reach the forest.

In the forest he could outflank the Bastard. He could stalk him. The advantage would be his. A person could never really know a forest, and knowing that fact would give the Old Man his much-needed edge. He climbed up over the boulders. Grass and a few weather-beaten logs separated him from the nearest trees. He started across the sand.

He realized his mistake too late to amend it. A bullet clipped his shin. The Old Man pitched forward, landing on the sand with the bag behind him. He kicked the bag back down into the rocks and lay quiet.

"Clever business with the lights," he heard the Bastard say.

Bullets punched the sand around him. The Old Man kept his head down the way a new soldier does who's unaccustomed to fire. He'd never seen the Bastard shoot. Was he missing on purpose to keep things interesting?

The Old Man needed to get back to his equipment bag, but that was impossible given that he was pinned down, with the Bastard closing in. He'd need to circle around. He could break for the forest, or he could slip into the water and approach from a different point. Swimming would tire him. Waiting here was no good. A forest run was suicide. He crawled ahead, judging the distance to the log. Paltry cover, but better than what he had now.

He did a soldier's spring to a standing position and ran all-out. When he reached the log, this strange surge of vitality carried him over it and he broke for the trees at a dead run.

He crashed into branches and fell to the dry mulch of the forest floor. Truthfully he couldn't recollect bullets chasing him, or the thundercrack of a rifle. The pain in his leg, the sweat beneath his coat, and his overworked synthetic heart—those were real. He could have dressed the wound with the kit in his bag, but his bag was wedged between boulders at the water's edge.

A network of well-trod paths led around the island. The Old Man could stay off the paths and trample through ivy and undergrowth, or chance the hard-packed dirt. Visibility versus noise. He stuck to the path.

He'd feint, as if to circle around the Bastard's position, and then double back for his bag. Without the bag he had no chance. He hoped the Bastard didn't know it. He had a folding knife in his pocket. The Bastard had a gun. Doubtless the Bastard had other things.

The flesh wound aggravated his stride, but didn't devolve into a limp. His footsteps were silent.

The ground rose. To his left was a still lake. A dancefloor of algae and fallen leaves rested on the stagnant water. To his right the trail led off to the bay named after the dead Hawaiian.

The Old Man thought about that story as he walked. The Hawaiian had been executed for murder, tried by the Hudson's Bay Company, in the days when the country was a trading post for the British. He wondered how fair the trial had been, a dark-skinned defendant in a company-run post. Maybe someone had taken a dislike to the Hawaiian. Maybe the Hawaiian had offended one of the merchants' daughters. To be buried in an unmarked grave on a strange island—he'd offended someone.

The ground sparked in front of him. Instinctively the Old Man dove, landing in a soft mess of fern and rotten wood. He started crawling away from the track, turning back to see where the shots were coming from. The sound was too soft for a large-caliber rifle.

Something landed nearby, something fused and burning. He rolled away as it exploded in a gasp of smoke.

Dummies. Firecrackers.

He looked up and saw the Bastard, belted into a hunting hide between two trees on the other side of the trail. He was bringing up his rifle. The Old Man leapt up and moved.

He ignored the pain. He was disoriented. He thought he was heading toward the water. He stumbled over a fallen tree. A bullet blasted away shards of rotten wood. The Old Man dove over, landed, scurried out of sight.

The Bastard was laughing.

Bullets chipped away at the Old Man's cover. He knew a well-placed shot could slam right through a dead tree. He dug in. He had a feeling the Bastard wanted him dug in.

He stayed there for an hour. If he tried to run, the Bastard would have a good sight on him. And what was in that direction—the water? What could he do there?

Why firecrackers? Why not grenades?

It was a game to the Bastard. Never a duel. The Old Man wasn't his equal. Hadn't been even before retirement. He was toying with him. Herding him towards--

He heard something hissing from the nearby foliage. Suddenly the air was redolent with an acrid, sour smell. The Old Man's eyes watered. Tear gas? Some kind of homemade agent?

His skin burned. He bolted from cover, stumbling. He heard the shots and thought he could hear the bullets passing him, swarms of them, one shot rolling into another.

He was running. He was sobbing. The chemicals burned his throat and nose. He could hear the water. He headed that way.

The ground sloped downward. He slid and stopped. Milky vision slowly returned to his eyes. When it did, he saw he was near the water's edge. The bottom of the short slope was lined with punji sticks, dozens of them, sticking out of the ground like brown serrated teeth. Coils of razor wire wound around their base. If he hadn't stopped, hadn't sensed something was off...

He realized what an idiot he'd been. He'd gone into this as a duel. The Bastard had spent the year arranging amusements for himself. *This* was the game for the Bastard—to make him run this obstacle course, the two of them, stalker and prey.

The Bastard would be behind him, with the rifle, waiting to finish him off.

The Old Man pulled out two of the punji sticks, broke one, tossed the top half and the other stick into the water. He jabbed the broken bottom half back into the mud, and used his hands to create the impression of a limb sliding into the water.

He took up the heaviest thing nearby, a segment of rotten stump, and heaved it into the lake. The splash was underwhelming and it bobbed in the water. But it had stirred up the silt below.

The Old Man scrambled back into the tree line, slowed his breathing, and waited.

He heard footfalls, the crunch of dry leaves. He didn't look up. The feet stopped. Leaves ruffled near where the Old Man lay. The Bastard was prodding the bushes, looking for traps. With a pained wheeze the Bastard made it down the bank. The Old Man looked up, saw the Bastard kneeling, holding up the broken stick. The Old Man stood up very quietly. He'd already opened the clasp on his blade.

One chance.

The Bastard was below him with his back to him. He took aim and threw. Instinctively the Bastard turned. He'd aimed for the Bastard's heart. The turn moved a shoulder into the blade's path. The blade cut into the Bastard. The Bastard fell. He landed on the razor wire and let out a whinny of a scream that would have been funny anywhere else.

The Old Man ran. It was at least two miles back to the rocks. The bag was everything. He could collapse of a stroke or heart failure after. He had to get the bag.

The Bastard had the gun. The Bastard would know the fastest way across the island. The Old Man was unarmed. If he wasn't fast enough…

Somewhere on the island the dead Hawaiian was buried. Which meant that with every step, he could be walking on someone's grave.

He stuck to the trail and didn't pause once for air, not until he was at the edge of the forest. He'd come out farther south than he'd planned. Here there was no grass, no driftwood between him and the rocks.

He started across the open ground. The first shot *pang*-ed across one of the boulders that lay so frustratingly close ahead. He ran all out. A shot tore through his shoulder and propelled him forward, onto the rocks.

He fell, pulling himself over, putting the boulders between him and the shooter. He edged close to where he'd kicked the bag.

The bag wasn't there. He reached over to probe the crevice where the bag had been, but his arm refused to move. He could feel precious blood soaking through his coat. He looked up.

The Bastard was crossing the beach at a casual pace, obviously in pain. The rifle was in his hands.

"You're cleverer than you were," he called out.

The Old Man ignored him. He turned over and used his good arm to feel about in the junctions between the rocks.

His fingers touched the woven nylon handle.

"Now that you've got your guns," the Bastard was saying, "we can escalate things a bit."

"Didn't bring a gun," the Old Man said. His good hand pulled the black weatherproof case from the bag, and he began undoing the clasps.

A desperate shot rang out, hitting the rocks. The Old Man was moving now, the device in his hands. With his teeth he pulled up the antenna.

"Spent the year learning about radio frequencies," the Old Man said. "Never could figure which one you used. Had to learn how to sweep through them. Technology's sure something."

He depressed the device's lone button and stood up. The Bastard had the rifle leveled at him.

The Bastard didn't shoot. The Bastard was laughing.

The Old Man's thumb left the button. He dropped and covered his head. The explosion shifted the boulders and raised the heat and left nothing of the Bastard except dark pieces of bone and gore amidst a spew of blood.

The noise was enough to break the skull.

It didn't stop, either. The Old Man felt a rumbling. He stood up. He watched a plume of fire leap out of the forest, then another, then more. A sequence of explosions, painting the sky black and red, detonating the island. The mine shafts. The Bastard had wired it all.

The boulders danced as the rocky beach went up in turn. The blast left fires that cooked everything in their wake.

The Old Man crouched and listened to the intermittent rumblings. The sand burned into glass and the trees gave way to geysers of fire and shattered earth. Pressure and terror seemed to meet and fuse. Black sleep rolled over him.

He dreamt of white raccoons.

Allure Furs
By Patti Abbott

I began working the counter at Allure Furs the September I was seventeen. I was tired of the lifestyle my measly allowance bought—fed up with being the "poor me" high school girl with no money for a Saturday night movie, a Bon Jovi concert, or a pair of Calvin Klein jeans. My mother—single and overworked—seemed relieved that I removing the burden of providing such things from her.

Few would have predicted a shop selling expensive fur coats could appear so down-on-its-heels, but Allure Furs managed it, squashed as it was between a dilapidated movie theater with a torn marquee showing second-run films, and a donut shop with a missing "u" in its sign, dating from the 1930's. *Dont*, as the sign spelled out in electric green letters, turned out to be a fitting warning. The trio of businesses attracted little interest except for an early morning sugar rush and the midnight Saturday showing of *The Rocky Horror Picture Show*. I was never around for either event.

Allure Furs had no reliable clientele, sometimes managing to elude customers for days. Standing at the bus stop at five o'clock, the incessant hum of the movie soundtracks still rang in my ears, and my clothes carried home the combined scents of popcorn, licorice and yeast. It took no small effort to remove the smell from my clothes.

My decision to apply for this job seemed flawed almost immediately when my prospective employer came out to meet me. Mr. Polifax was the most hairless man I'd ever seen, and he walked with his midsection thrust out, the rest of him following behind in a slithery crawl. Physically, there was nothing to admire and more importantly, his personality was no better than his countenance.

"Are you sure you can be here by two on weekdays and ten on Saturdays?" Mr. Polifax asked at my interview, brushing the omnipresent yet non-existent hair from his face for the tenth time. "No personal phone calls, no boyfriends visiting?"

Twice, he'd put a hand on my arm, the last time several inches above the elbow. I managed to hide my revulsion well enough to be hired on the spot, learning later I'd been the only one to apply. But Mr. Polifax employed me with the reluctance of a man who'd purchased a bobcat and we gave each other a wide berth as much as possible. He was on the road buying and selling coats much of time. As for me, working the counter at Allure Furs seemed like a better idea than hawking pizzas or filing library books—the sorts of employment my mother had suggested.

My duties included manning the front counter, answering the phone, ringing up sales—mostly from storage fees and the occasional purchase of accessories—never for something as consequential as a coat. The sale of even a muff was reason for excitement.

After the first few weeks, I brought a paperback along. Hours passed without a single customer coming into the shop. The storage fees must carry the business, I decided—or perhaps large sales took place on the frequent trips Mr. Polifax took. Once or twice, I spotted invoices for furs sold, but those were rare.

"I bet he's laundering money," a friend suggested.

I was too embarrassed to admit I didn't know what that meant. Never again would I enjoy such innocence.

"Iris."

It was Mr. Polifax, coming out of the backroom in a rush. I jumped, not knowing he was back there, and slid *Flowers In The Attic* under the counter. "Lisa's down with the flu. I wondered if you might step in for her tomorrow."

Lisa was the older girl Allure Furs employed for customers who asked to see a fur modeled or for the runway show Polifax mounted twice a year. She was a skinny blonde who wore too much makeup, staggeringly high heels, and fancied herself the next Elle Macpherson. She seldom deigned to talk to me, preferring the petting she received at the hands of Mr. Polifax and Myrtle and already sported the world-weary look of a middle-aged woman.

"A customer's coming in late this afternoon. Lisa usually handles it but..." Mr. Polifax looked at me critically. "Can you do something with your hair, Iris? Maybe put it up? No, it's probably too short for that," he said, running a hand across the nape of my neck. Every hair stood on end as if commanded. "I've never understood why young girls cut off their hair. Well anyway, ask Myrtle for some advice." He motioned with his head toward the backroom, and then paused, a hand on his hip. "Try to look like Audrey Hepburn in *Breakfast at Tiffany's*. You might bring that off. Do you know who she is?"

I nodded.

"Good," he said. "That's the kind of look we strive for. Classy."

I tried not to glance at the dandruff on his lapels, the worn cuffs on his shirt, the scuffed tips of his burgundy Thom McAn loafers.

"Go see what Myrtle can do with you." His hand darted just to the left of my backside before he glided away. Even the air his movement produced was repulsive.

Though Myrtle's wildly permed hair and penchant for wearing jewelry made from shells, bird feathers, and fish skeletons was hardly a selling point for beauty advice, I walked into the back room, a place where Myrtle spent her days performing the miraculous bookkeeping tricks that kept Allure Furs afloat. She seemed clueless, suspicious, and ruthless all at once. We'd never had a conversation beyond a discussion of the weather, her cat Lamour, and how I should fill out various forms.

"A wig would probably be the best way to go," Myrtle said, spinning around in the desk chair. "Can't do much with that pixie-cut you favor. Glamour needs more volume. Selling furs is easier if they're modeled by a sexy girl. Men wanted to think their wives will look gorgeous if they buy them a fur. It's your job to make them believe it. Now, what can we do with you?"

This was by far the longest speech Myrtle had ever made to me. And here I was, within a scant two minutes, receiving fashion advice from a person who looked like an extra for an episode of *Alfred Hitchcock Presents*. I held my tongue. Maybe there'd be more money in modeling because Lisa certainly seemed well-fed and dressed.

Reaching over with a frown, Myrtle yanked open a file drawer, pulled out a ratty-looking auburn wig, and tossed it to me. In the split-second before I caught it, it appeared a ferret was headed my way. I could smell Aquanet hairspray, disturbed from its years of rest, and possibly something else.

"Of course, you'll have to play with it, tease it, plump it up. Give it a little flair. Why don't you take it home? Practice on it. You might even throw it in some Woolite and let it soak for an hour or two. Woolite can do wonders."

Unconsciously, Myrtle's right hand went to her own head. "I've been known to pull a wig on in a pinch. I may even have worn that one once or twice. Not so many years ago, it was me modeling furs for Mr. P."

I beat back the impulse to drop it on the floor. It was the faint but noxious scent of Myrtle's favorite perfume that was coming through along with the Aquanet. Or perhaps the odor of the back office itself, pickled in Charlie after all of Myrtle's years at Allure Furs. Mr. Polifax kept her as far from the furs as possible. And even farther from the customers.

I returned later that day, wig in place, makeup on, the highest heels Payless sold jammed on my feet.

"Well, that's more like it," Mr. Polifax said, coming out of the back room. "Who'd guess you'd clean up this good? Might sell a coat today after all." He circled me. "The added height's terrific. You must top six feet in those shoes."

He was flush with approval, and when the customer bought an expensive mink an hour later, Mr. Polifax was ecstatic. "Good work, Iris. You got the knack." Actually I had gotten off a bit on the show I put on (to my surprise)—walking back and forth on the little ramp Mr. Polifax called his runway. And I did seem to have the knack for it. The guy had me model furs for almost a half-hour and then bought the second one I had worn. I listened to him with a smile pasted on my face when he told me he could get me a deal on a used Buick if I came down to his lot. I took the card he held out and smiled even wider. This might really work out.

Lisa and I began sharing the modeling duties. "You know when to shut your trap," Mr. Polifax said, in a rare attempt at a compliment. "Lisa likes to chat up the customers. Sometimes it works, but…"

It was several weeks later that he asked me to come in on a Friday night. "This guy can only make it after eight," he said, running a nervous hand through his non-existent hair. I wondered if the gesture looked less absurd when his hand had swept through hair rather than air, but I took the gesture itself for a worrisome sign. Just who was this guy coming in at night? And why was it freaking Mr. Polifax out?

I was somewhat relieved when he added, "Could mean a big sale for us so I'm reluctant to turn it over to that big-mouthed Lisa. This customer's the silent type." He squinted as he licked his thumb and flipped through his Rolodex. "Your mother works Friday nights, right?" He was looking at the card with my name on it now. "Well, I can give you a ride home. It's practically right on my way."

Ugh. Would the nastiness of Allure Furs never end? I imagined him cruising my house in the ancient VW bus he drove to cart furs around. "Nobody expects to find fur coats in a piece of junk like this," he explained.

Friday night, I tried on a lynx and a karakul lamb coat for a tiny man who never said a word. He looked at me or the coat—take your choice—from under barely opened eyelids. After the lynx, Mr. Polifax came hurrying into the back room.

"Look, Iris—just the coat, never mind the rest."

I must have had my mouth open because he added, "Leave your clothing back here. You know." He looked me up and down as if I'd already stripped. I could actually feel my clothes falling away in his eyes.

"What would be the point of that?" I said, watching him in the mirror. It wasn't like my skimpy dress was making the coat fall unevenly. It had no effect on the fur at all. I struggled to make sense of it.

Mr. Polifax turned a bright pink. "This client—well, he's a little odd—but he'll probably buy something or make it worth our while if he gets a peek."

A peek? A peek at what?

"Look, Lisa does it all the time. Well, not all the time maybe, but now and then. I would've thought she'd filled you in on it. I'm sure I told her to bring you up to speed.

Or maybe it was Myrtle I told to talk to you." He paused and when I didn't say anything, continued, "Some men—well, some of then—they like a little show. It greases the wheels for a sale. Harmless stuff really." He giggled.

I shook my head and he sighed.

"Look, there'll be something extra in your paycheck next week. Be a good girl and show him the goods."

The goods. What were the goods?

"What if I do it and he still doesn't buy a coat? I'll still get the extra pay?" I wasn't the fool he took me for. "I'll get something extra even if he doesn't buy a fur? Right?" I repeated more firmly. Any girl in her right mind wouldn't even be considering this stunt, so I might as well push any thoughts of virtue aside. I had "the goods" and he wanted "the goods." I wasn't sure what kind of money we were talking about but it had to be the price of a pair of jeans at the very least.

Mr. Polifax paused again, and then nodded.

"And no touching me, right? He has to keep his grubby little hands to himself!" I was hardly going to allow that nasty man in the other room to put his hands on me.

"Okay, no touching. I'll be right there, Iris. But if you take such a prissy, superior attitude out there, he won't buy anything and our little arrangement will end. Lisa's been trying to get me to give her more hours." He blinked twice. "She's very amenable to client requests. She's a smart one, that Lisa."

His lips disappeared as he straightened his back, clearly annoyed, and he pushed open the door and left me alone.

The little man was standing in the same spot when I walked out of the back room wearing a hugely expensive sable that only someone my height could pull off. He gave no indication that either it or me was anything special, remaining mostly mute and using his hands to indicate certain moves he wanted me to make. It looked like he was conducting an invisible orchestra. I followed his instructions almost like an automaton—never fully disrobing, but certainly modeling more than the coat.

The show, or whatever it was, went on for about ten minutes, and it wasn't an entirely dissatisfying experience. I enjoyed watching myself in the full-length mirrors circling the room. The fractured pieces of me, the swirling coat, the man's face, all crisscrossing the room. A kaleidoscope of images. I was getting better at it all the time, and I can't say the strange sort of power I wielded over this man didn't have its reward. The way his features seem to slide off his face and turn to liquid. Desire. That was what it was.

At the end of the show, the small man's face quickly lost that waxy, liquidy texture and returned to an almost featureless look—stony and fixed. I might have never disrobed at all from his placid appearance. But Mr. Polifax was visibly panting, seemingly ill-equipped to show the customer to the door.

When the door closed, Mr. Polifax sank into the nearest chair and fanned himself. "You did good, Iris," he said. "You're a born model. We're gonna make some money—you and me."

My little ballet netted an extra $75 in my next check, almost doubling what I made most weeks. I now understood how Allure Furs stayed in business despite its poor sales. It was a strip club. A strip club for private customers. Seedier even than the ones I heard about across the Detroit River in Windsor. Places where desperate men sought relief from their loneliness and bad marriages.

My check grew over the next weeks even if my self-respect did not. If virtue was its own reward, a lack of virtue paid well too. The performance became rote and my initial interest in the men and their faces waned. I felt like a prostitute and would've denied I did such a thing to even my closest friends. Various unpleasant circumstances arose too. Men whispering words like "slut" under their breath; men masturbating while they watched me; men taking photographs of me wearing a mask if they ponied up enough money, men panting, sighing, and in one case, crying.

Gradually, Mr. Polifax treated me differently too. Although the men didn't touch my body, they'd touched something deeper and it became harder and harder to live with it. By day I was a virginal seventeen-year-old; by night I was a stripper in the sleaziest club on earth.

It ended in the way you might expect.

One night, well after closing hour, a man I'd never seen before entered the shop for an appointment. I should have been suspicious because Mr. Polifax had been on pins and needles all day, opening and closing drawers, multiple trips to his private john, rearranging coats, mumbling, hushed conversations on the telephone. Another thing that should have tipped me off me was Lisa had backed out of the night's job when she saw the client's name in the appointment book. She covered it up by saying this fellow went to her church and she couldn't risk him recognizing her. As soon as I saw him I knew this guy had never seen the inside of any church.

"Iris—this guy, this guy," Mr. Polifax stuttered, in the moments before the client entered the shop, "well, he likes a little contact. Nothing too fancy but—well he really pays well. I can probably pay you double the usual rate."

"But more or less the usual?"

"More or less."

But Mr. Polifax didn't look me in the eye.

The man who entered the back room a few minutes later topped 6'4. But his width or girth was even more impressive than his height. He looked like Bluto in the *Popeye* comics. An acid wash began swirling in my stomach. Most of the guys I'd modeled for were either jokey or solemn in a creepy way. But this guy, this monster of a man, had a look of venom on his face—just like Bluto, in fact. He saw me for what I'd become and intended to take advantage of it.

"Iris, if you need me, I'll be in the next room."

Before I could protest Mr. Polifax's quick exit, Bluto had slammed the door shut with his heel.

"That's not our arrangement," I shouted. "You're supposed to…"

The client put his mammoth hand over my mouth. "You don't need to say another word," he whispered. "And don't pretend to be an innocent kid either. Some guys like that kinda stuff—but not me."

A smile crept up his face as he pushed me up against a mirror and raised his knee, knocking my shaking knees apart. There was no way I was going anywhere. His mouth, lips large and livery, was on my neck, and his breath was both hot and fetid. His other hand, ham-fisted and awkward, searched for my breast. Finding it, he squeezed hard enough to make a scream leak out from behind his other hand. He was surprised, and I used that moment to raise my foot sharply. Using the heel, I broke the mirror behind me. The shattering glass brought Mr. Polifax back into the room within seconds.

"Hey," he said, looking Bluto in the face. "What do you think you're doing in here? That glass cost good money." Then he noticed me cowering in the corner. "You okay, Iris?" I was shaking too hard to answer.

"Look," Bluto said, and he was looking at me. "Don't give me any of that stuff, girly. How'd you like it if a piece of the glass under my foot found its way to your face? That'd put an end to your little shell game. A few guys out there like scars, but not enough to make it worth hiring you."

But before his hand reached the floor, Mr. Polifax pulled a gun from his jacket pocket. He was far less awkward with the weapon than I'd have expected.

"Time to go, friend. Ten seconds and I pull the trigger."

"What're you trying to pull, you four-flushing fairy," the man said "You know what I come here for. Same thing as always. What's-her-name knows the score. Where's she tonight?"

But Mr. Polifax said nothing as the gun inched higher. I heard the sound of a hammer being pulled back. Bluto was out the door in seconds.

"Sorry 'bout that, Iris," Mr. Polifax said once we heard the door close. "It'll never happen again. I guarantee it." He put the gun back in his pocket, wiped his sweating face. "Sometimes... unfortunate...*things* like this happen." When I said nothing, he drove me home. "Lisa knows how to handle him," he said at the curb. "I suppose you're out of...things, after this."

I got out of the car without answering.

A month or two later, the trio of stores anchored by Allure Furs burned to the ground in a spectacular blaze. You could smell the odor of an accelerant mixed with burning pastry, animal skins, and acetate along with other chemicals used in screening movies. The Fire Marshal couldn't decide whether it was the faulty projector at the theater or the oven at the donut shop that caused it. Although the fire was at night, both Mr. Polifax and a client were on the premises and perished in what was called an extremely rapid-moving fire. Myrtle called to give me the news although she needn't have bothered. Fortunately, or unfortunately, depending on your point of view, neither man died—at least not right away.

My mother threw the newspaper on the table at breakfast. "Looks like you got out of that place just in time, Iris."

I wondered if she could smell it on me. Not just the chemicals but all of it.

Of Being Darker Than Light
by Garrett Crowe

Before he was blue-lighted, Rex sped by the road lines so fast they turned into one long surveyor-yellow tightrope that only he and his motorcycle were brave enough to balance across. The speed turned him into a blur, a transparent ghost flying down empty roads. He had just left Snow White's Bar after knocking some Young Boy out.

Everything starts slow in the beginning, so when he saw the blue strobe, Rex stopped the bike as quickly as he could. It gave him enough time to pull the leather pouch from his jacket pocket and give an underhand toss. The pouch arced into the tree line, Mile Marker 7. He'd come back tomorrow.

When the white Chevy Impala pulled behind him, the vehicle's blue strobe and headlights lit the scene. There was Rex covered in homemade tattoos of the finest dirty-kitchen quality. He wore a sleeveless denim jacket with *$3 SOULS* embroidered on the back in champion-yellow and had a head full of soap-hating black hair. And then there were the two police officers that got out of the car. One was older, shorter, and broader than the other.

The older one said, "Where you going? The moon?" His partner didn't say anything. "If this was Memphis, there'd be guns drawn." They got on each side of the motorcycle. The older one continued, "Have I had run-ins with you before?"

He had. The older cop was Jerry Powers, and when Rex was a teenager, he once rode in the back of Jerry's cop car after being caught trying to steal beer from the Little General convenience store. He remembered the car's radio tuned to the oldies station, the volume so low he could only make out the choruses. He also remembered how the night lights of the town rolled in the dark backseat. On the way to the police department, the officer glanced in the rear-view mirror, trying to talk sense to the sixteen-year old. The standard lecture; "What's your family going to think about this? Better straighten up because I know exactly where you're headed if you don't."

But that was almost ten years ago, and Rex knew by Jerry's face he didn't remember. "Don't believe we've met," Rex said.

"Well, license, registration, proof of insurance?" Jerry asked. Rex pulled the information from his wallet. The officer didn't look at it and handed it to his partner. "Tip, run that for me."

Rex didn't know Tip. The younger officer was tall with buzzed dark hair. Unlike Jerry, his forehead was free of wrinkles. Rex could tell Tip hadn't been with the J.P.D. for long by the way he had followed Jerry out of the car and waited for his partner to talk. He didn't even rest his hand on his holster like Jerry had.

Rex looked at Tip's badge, the Jackson Police bald eagle with its open-mouth and unfurled wings in the blinking blue lights. Underneath the badge, a nametag that read Ofc. Carrington in engraved letters. Rex knew a Carrington from somewhere, but the name lost itself as Tip went back to the vehicle, leaving Jerry and Rex alone. Jerry walked in circles around the motorcycle. The hand that wasn't resting on the gun holster carried a flashlight that surveyed the bike like a silver baton, the light traveling between the crannies of the engine, muffler, and spokes.

"Why you going so fast?" Jerry asked.

"Didn't realize I was," Rex said, but he knew he had been. The longer he drove the faster he accelerated. Sometimes he imagined being in a race with his father's '69 Pontiac GTO. Richard Fowler called it The Goat, already a classic by the time Rex was born. Taking night-rides with his father as a boy, Rex tried counting the yellow rectangles that lay in the road, but he could never get a good count going. His father simply drove too fast. While Richard raced beyond 60 miles per hour, and then beyond 70 miles per hour, Rex could only get to numbers like thirteen or fourteen before the markings passed him at speeds faster than he could count, a pace beyond memory and comprehension. Rex would give up, the velocity of The Goat taking his mind elsewhere.

However, those rides only happened on occasion. When Richard was in one of his rare moods, he'd ask his son to take a ride, and without a thought, Rex always went.

Richard brought his son outside the city limits. "The cops don't really care out here," he said. And in that country darkness, trees became another component of the night, another shade of black. Rex's father pressed down on the gas pedal, and the Goat's engine yelled violence at deafening levels. The father tightened his hands around the steering wheel, gripping it so hard his only tattoo on his right shoulder moved. The tattoo depicted a cobra striking a panther. When he wore sleeveless tops, his son watched the snake stir with wrath against the cat. And if Richard got really excited, he screamed with the engine, "*It's the speed that matters. The speed.*" Rex nodded, giving a weak smile.

But those memories of his father were the only ones Rex remotely appreciated. He had come to believe that when he was a growing boy, his father couldn't accept being grown. Richard was rarely home. And if he was home, he didn't pay much attention to BeBe or Rex.

BeBe had told her son that when Richard clocked out of his factory job, where he manufactured car door handles for Toyota, he wandered off to other places. "He likes going to John-Ray's," she said, "where he smokes pot from a glass bong and enjoys feeling trashy." When BeBe was pregnant with Rex, she had told her husband no more of that in the house, so Richard went elsewhere.

She also claimed Richard dined in bars where he took a few sips and let strange women borrow both a cigarette and a light. "But he don't go to places like the Drink Box or the Fishing Pond to just beer-up and talk to women," she said. "He likes visiting those places because of the attention his GTO gets. He thinks when he pulls up in the parking lot with the engine cranking in demon power, all the bartenders and barstoolees say, 'There's Richie Fowler, hollering at hell.' Or when he leaves, 'There's Richie, rip roaring away.' He thinks people want to watch The Goat's red paintjob go in and out of sight from the parking lot."

But most of the time, Richard didn't go to any of those places. When he came home on those nights, he didn't smell like John-Ray's sweet leaf, nor did he have the attached film of bar smoke on his factory-blue overalls. He smelled like nothing.

"Where you been?" BeBe asked, while Rex hid in the hallway and listened.

"Nowhere," Richard replied.

Rex imagined Nowhere being a place where everything was much different than home. Nowhere had no edges or boundaries. His father drove his GTO in a planet of black and anti-everything, like one of those motorcycle cage-spheres made out of steel he had seen in movies. And instead of a dirt bike, his father drove the GTO forwards, backwards, down, up, left, right, diagonally, and in other directions too. All in darkness. Nowhere was where Richard truly wanted to be, where he was truly happy, where he was truly himself. And when Rex was thirteen, it was where his father went when Richard suddenly packed his bags, left in his car, and never came back to BeBe or Rex again.

*****

Jerry kept walking in slow circles around the motorcycle. He had stopped shining the flashlight on the bike and put it to Rex's body, the orb rotating around his chest, arms, and back.

"Where you coming from?"

Rex wasn't about to lie just yet. "The bar. Only had one and a half before you ask."

Jerry stopped walking and shined the flashlight into Rex's eyes. "Which bar?"

"Snow White's." Rex began to squint.

"Light hurting your eyes?" the officer asked. He brought the flashlight down and saw the tattoos on Rex's hands. "What in the hell's on your knucks?" The cop picked up Rex's hands and read the tattoos aloud, "An Upside Down Star, E, A, T, G, O, D, Upside Down Cross." Jerry made a sound with his tongue and continued, "What drives you to put something like that on your body?"

Rex didn't say anything.

"Well, I tell you what's interesting," the officer said, letting go of the tattooed hands. "It's interesting you coming from the bar. We just heard a call about Snow White's on the radio. You know what I'm talking about?"

"Don't have a clue."

"Don't know anything about a fight?"

"No fight happened while I was there."

"Yeah? There was a fight sure enough. A report that some kid got it good," Jerry said. "By a biker."

"That's something."

"Something alright. You're coming from a biker bar. And you're a biker. I ain't fooled, I know what a Three Dollar Soul is," he alluded to the patch on Rex's back. "I know you fashion yourselves a motorcycle club," he said. "Coincidence is something."

"I wasn't the only biker there. I didn't see a fight. I haven't thrown a punch all night, and I ain't got nothing for you," Rex said. However, he had seen the fight...real good.

Who knows how it got started. One of the Young Boys could've said something smart to Pettin, K.J. or Killer Juice, Endless Frank, or any of the Three Dollar Souls. Maybe Big Cody threw a beer at one of the Young Boys for getting too close. Or maybe it was none of that. Perhaps a wind came into the bar, pushing smoke from any of the numerous lit cigarettes in the face of T-Boy who hated the smell of "that bullshit", which in turn made him mad as a hornet and ready to start something with any of the cocky-shit Young Boys playing a game of darts adjacent to the Three Dollar Souls' pool table. It wasn't that difficult to get a fight started in Snow White's on a Friday night with the Three Dollar Souls.

"Oh, shit. You knocked him cucumber-cold," Pettin said as he came from behind, shaking Rex by the shoulder. Everyone knew that when one falls like that it's over. "You boys came on the wrong night." He started dancing around with his right middle finger in the air and his left hand on his crotch. "Y'all didn't know Rex here got the fist from Hell."

Rex watched the Young Boys drag their friend out the door, the boy's feet pointing to the ceiling like a body in a morgue.

"Anyone got a toe tag?" Pettin asked as if he read Rex's mind.

The Young Boys weren't a motorcycle club like the Three Dollar Souls. They weren't a neighborhood gang either. They were only called the Young Boys because that's what they were—young boys. Boys that just graduated high school and came to Snow White's on weekends for the 75 cent-a-game pool tables, the jukebox that played anything from Merle Haggard to Danzig, and the bar-mothers who might just partake in serving a minor if the boys "acted nice."

Five of them came into Snow White's on this particular night, all wearing tight t-shirts that showed off their youthful weight-bench biceps. Rex watched them walk around with their chests cocked and shoulders wobbling. He knew the night would end with dramatics because the Three Dollar Souls didn't stand for Young Boys acting like Big Boys.

Before the fight started, Rex was sitting at the bar by himself until Pettin came along from the pool table. Pettin was a long-time member of the Three Dollar Souls and Rex's roommate.

"Them Young Boys ready for some stuff tonight," he said.

Rex nodded. "They usually are. What'd they do?"

"Saying it was their turn for the pool table."

"But there are two pool tables."

"That's what I told them, but they said we knew damn well the one we were on was the flattest. Just horseshit, you know." He began laughing, "And when they dribbled that mess, fucking Big Cody, straight-faced as a metal pole, said, 'Looks like y'all gotta get a new set of rules then.'"

"What'd they say back to Cody?" Rex asked

"Nothing. Probably mumbled out their ass." Pettin waved his hand to alert Vickie the bartender. Rex smelled the combination of leather and body odor from Pettin while he moved.

Vickie came over, grinning, and said, "What you want, sonbitch?"

"Damn, woman. Always got something smart to say, don't she?"

"Don't I know, could barely get this," Rex said, holding up his beer.

"Oh, don't turn on me. I pay attention to you." And she did. They had a thing for each other that hadn't come to fruition, partly because Rex wasn't good at flirting. They were getting there though.

"But when I deal with the likes of him," Vickie pointed at Pettin, "I gotta be smart. Now what you want?"

"Bad bitch," Pettin said. He looked behind the bar, searching for something. "I want uhhh…"

"We ain't got Uhhh," Vickie said with the snap of a comedian.

"You're on one tonight. Just get me a Bud L."

"What about you?" she asked Rex.

"I'll take another," Rex said. Vickie nodded and gave him one of those winks that said the beer was free.

"Boy, that bird's got something for you," Pettin said.

"I don't know about that."

"You don't, but I do. Her red-hair and freckles shake when she talks to you. You'll be the stud of the parking lot if you get that. Ready for a girlfriend?"

Rex looked Pettin dead in the face and said, "You're nuthouse crazy."

"Which means yes. I ain't ever known you with a girl before, but you ready."

Rex had had women, but only the type with faded tattoos down their thighs and skin sun-colored to the likes of a penny. Biker Bitches, that's what they were called. Those types of women were always around, and neither Rex, nor anyone else in the club, wanted a Biker Bitch as a girlfriend, significant other, or wife. Maybe as a pet, but that's about it.

Vickie was different though. He didn't think she'd ever been with a biker before, and he imagined her coming to his apartment after a long night at Snow White's. And when she came home from work, he'd ask if she had enough energy to go for a ride. She would. She'd put on her helmet and jacket he had bought for her and sit behind him on his bike. He'd feel her breasts on his back, her leather-sleeves wrapped around his leather-torso like a nut and a bolt. And he'd go fast, but they'd do it together, so fast that the gravity tried to pull her away from him, her arms trying to slip off his waist while the motorcycle's speed pulled faster and stronger than gravity could take and---

"Here y'all go," Vickie said, pulling the tab for each of their beers. The can's lip made a hollow sound when it cracked. "I'll check back in a bit."

But it wasn't long after Vickie served the beer that everyone heard "Hey! Hey, hey!" coming from the pool tables. Rex turned and saw T-Boy, Big Cody, Endless Frank, and the rest of the Souls grabbing the Young Boys' shirts, throats, and arms.

Without thinking twice, Rex went straight into the thrall of youthful muscles and biker tattoos. He pushed and punched until he squared evenly with one of the younger Young Boys. The showdown didn't last long because Rex went off first, slamming his tattooed fist into smooth chin. The Young Boy fell like a shoddy bomb. But it wasn't just the punch. It was the way he smacked against the floor too. On the way down, his arms, legs, and spine were already stiffed by the blow, so when the Young Boy hit ground, his hands didn't break the fall. His head sounded like a baseball hitting a field made of concrete. Rex had heard rumors of people dying like that.

*****

"So you're telling me you don't know anything about a fight?" Jerry asked.

"That's what I'm telling."

"Okay then."

"Don't believe me? Hell, take me to Snow White's. Get what you call an I D," Rex said.

"Think I don't know how it works up there? All of you, the Dollared Souls, the bartenders, the patrons, thicker than a tribe. Ain't worth the time."

Rex knew he didn't have to worry about the Young Boys either, too cocky to report an ass-whooping.

"Looks like my partner's getting out of the car now though," Jerry said.

Tip walked towards the two, staring at Rex and shaking his head. Rex was reminded again of Tip's last name—Carrington. Once more he tried to grasp where he knew it from, the name clear in his head. He saw it spelled perfectly clean, yet it was like the bottom of the letters had roots. Roots that went deep, but eventually connected together in the deepest of layers. He'd have to dig get it.

"Cheryl looked. Nothing on him," Tip said, handing the information back to Jerry.

"We'll see." Jerry studied the driver's license and said, "Rex Fowler? I do know you. When you were younger, you tried to steal a Corona from the store on Huntingdon that ain't there no more." He turned to Tip. "I remember because it wasn't liquor, wasn't cigarettes, and out of all the beers in the world, a single Corona. I still think about it every now and then. Why didn't you say anything, Rex?"

"Who said I remembered you?"

Jerry gave a laugh. "True." He went back to the license. "Got a birthday coming too. You'll be what, twenty-six?"

Rex nodded his head, looking off somewhere.

"Tip, what you think of all this tattoo and biker stuff?"

"Oh hell, Jerry, I don't know," he responded as if scared of giving the wrong opinion.

Disappointed in Tip's response, the older officer went back to Rex. "So when'd you join this rag-tag crew of yours?"

"Eighteen" Rex said, a year after he dropped out of school. BeBe had tried to set him straight. She told him what an education could do, talked about actions and consequences, tried saying that life's a slot-machine and there's only so many quarters. BeBe said all these things to Rex, but he paid her no mind. Destroying school property led to fistfights at the ballpark, and fighting turned into stealing beers from the Little General. Indian-ink tattoos started showing up on his forearms. BeBe couldn't do anything for him. She got tired of trying.

A little before joining the Souls, Rex got a job as a dishwasher at Bailey's Southern. He still lived with his mother and had no bills to pay, so he saved every paycheck. BeBe thought it was a good sign—responsibility. And four months later, he scoped the BuySell section of the newspaper and saw an ad for a 91 Honda Nighthawk. Black. Only one rider before. Great-shape, $2000-FIRM. Rex got the bike for $1,500, his first motorcycle. He quit his job the next day.

Rex dedicated every minute to learning how to ride the bike, how to lean with the curves and bend his body against the wind. He wasn't afraid to try and pass the 110 mph marker either, where the speedometer quit counting because it was scared of going beyond. He mostly rode at night when the back roads were deserted. He'd come home early morning, get a bite to eat, and go to sleep.

Once he had a dream he was pulled over on the side of the road with nothing around him, no trees, no dirt, no ground, just the road with yellow lines that glowed a little bit, the only light. And then something in factory overalls with a black ram's head appeared. It may have been there the whole time. It had tall jagged horns that curved at the top. It pointed at Rex's bike and said, "That ain't gonna cut it," sounding like something that came from another dimension. "No American Muscle," it said. Then it went away, but the bricks on the road kept glowing.

There was more of nothing in the dream until his father's GTO appeared. No one was behind the wheel, but Rex could feel the car hating him. It let him know by the way its spark plugs, pistons, gears, rods, and belts exploded in single moments of combustion, moving together in a melody of infinite violence. It got so loud, Rex thought he'd go deaf. Finally, the car blasted forward, leaving him on the side of the road with his Nighthawk, watching the taillights go deeper and deeper until any semblance of the Goat completely disappeared, the dream ending.

Some nights while driving around, he'd pass Snow White's. He knew it was the home of the Three Dollar Souls. They'd been talked about and mythologized as long as Rex could remember. However, he heard conflicting reports about the motorcycle club. Once riding with his dad as a boy, they drove by the bar, and when his father saw the motorcycles, he said, "The Souls wouldn't know manhood if it punched them in the ass." But when Rex was still in high school, his classmates said the opposite. They'd claim the motorcycle club was a bunch of fighting badasses; "I know a guy that got stabbed by one over a card game," they said. So when he had his own bike and saw the flock of motorcycles in Snow White's parking lot, he believed his classmates.

Rex went inside Snow White's one night and walked up to the first leather jacket he saw, Big Cody, a biker with a forehead proportionate to a pit bull's and shoulders like a professional wrestler.

"Who do I need to talk to about joining the Three Dollar Souls?" Rex asked.

Big Cody looked at Rex from the tip of his boots to his long black hair and said, "Boy, this barstool's older than you."

"Who do I gotta talk to?"

"Talk to me, talk to him," he pointed at T-Boy, "talk to Pettin, talk to any of us. Hell, there ain't no leader in the Souls. But they all going to laugh at you like I'm about to if you keep at it." Big Cody turned away, but Rex kept standing there, making it awkward until the member asked how old he was.

"Eighteen in two months."

Big Cody sniffed something invisible. "You even got a bike?"

"A Honda Nighthawk," Rex said.

The biker gave a thunderous honk of a laugh that got everyone's attention. "It's best you learn that loud pipes save lives," he said. "And I guarantee your Honda sounds like a cat farting, but a Harley..." Big Cody got up from the table and into Rex's face with a quickness that had scared many men and women. He made the noise of a fiendish motorcycle engine, screaming like a hungry bear. While yelling, he shook his whole face and let beer-slobber slap against the collar of his jacket. Atoms of it touched Rex's checks, but he didn't flinch or wipe it off.

When Big Cody was done shaking his face, Rex said, "I'll get one when I can." And he kept standing there.

*****

"I want to say there used to another Fowler around here," Jerry said, "a little younger than me. He had a Pontiac that raised hell. You kin to him? Can't think of his name." Just as Jerry said that, Rex's memory sparked like a match. In that moment, he dug straight to the spot where all the roots connected into one piece below the surface. He saw it fully, comprehending it at all angles.

Carrington.

Carrington.

Ignoring Jerry's question, Rex turned to Tip and asked, "You know a Marcie Carrington? Up in Dyersberg?"

Tip said, "Yeah, she's my aunt. Mother's sister," spooked that Rex seemed to know her.

"What's that got to do with anything I'm asking you?" Jerry said.

"Just wondering," Rex replied. It had something to do with it. After joining the Three Dollar Souls, the entire club began treating Rex like an older son or younger brother. They introduced him to women. They tattooed him with homemade guns. They told him to remove the exhaust baffles and front fender off his Nighthawk. "You can get the shit-stock off at least," Big Cody said. "Make it louder. And it'll lose weight." They even got him a job.

"You want to deal?" Pettin had brought Rex over to his apartment. In a corner of the living room were two plastic storage-containers filled with pills in plastic baggies. "Am-fet-uh-means, can't sell them fast enough."

"I could do that," Rex said.

"Stay here then. I got an extra room. I'll make sure you get run-around money." Rex was in good.

He didn't go around his mother's that often, bored with the place and the parent he grew up with. But a week before turning twenty-two, he got a phone call from her, saying he needed to swing by.

BeBe sat in the kitchen, holding a letter. "Heard you pull up," she said. Rex slumped in the chair beside her. "Got this letter in the mail." She put it on the table and scooted the pages toward her son.

Rex didn't glance at it. "What is it?" he asked.

"You going to read it, or you want me to tell you?"

"Looks like you already read it."

"It's a letter from a woman named Marcie Carrington." BeBe got up from the table. Before she said anything else, she got herself a glass of ice water. "She lives in Dyersburg and says your father's dead." She sat back down at the table, drinking from the glass. The ice and the water jingled like a chime when she put it to her mouth. Rex watched light go inside the cup and come out in a prism of colors.

"He didn't go nowhere," Rex said.

"What?" his mother said, confused.

Rex shook his head and moved his hand as if back-handing a fly. "Okay then, I came out here for that?" he asked.

"Yeah, you did. But that ain't it." She took another sip. "This Marcie says Richie left you the GTO. It's at her house and wants you to come get it."

Rex made a sound with his voice, a beat of sound that came out cynical. He looked at his mother's hands wrapped around the sweating glass of water. The air-conditioner kicked on. He thought about what the Ram's head had told him in his dream. Rex stood up, grabbed the hand-written letter, and mashed it in his jacket pocket.

"What're you going to do with it?" his mother asked, tired of waiting for a response.

"I suppose I'll sell it."

*****

"Well, Rex, I think you need to hop off that Harley of yours," Jerry said. Rex got off the seat of the 883 Sportster. "Now turn around, spread your legs, put your hands up. There you go. Tip," Jerry pointed to the tree line, "look around over there. Make sure Mr. Fowler didn't drop something."

Jerry patted Rex down, his hands landing in sync on Rex's sides. "You got anything in your pockets? If it's pocket knives, pencils, or pills, I need to know about it." Rex shook his head. He watched Tip move his flashlight in frontward and backward lines. Rex thought it was difficult to see leather at night. The officer got closer and closer to the tree line while Jerry dug in Rex's jacket and pants. He went into each pocket, hoping to find something. Tip was at the tree line. Rex watched his hands. He hoped the flashlight wouldn't stop moving, that the officer kept going as if giving paint strokes of light to the ground. "Well, ain't nothing in your pockets." Rex thought about saying I told you so, but he hadn't told the officer anything. Rex watched Tip instead. Officer Carrington was right there, moving the slither of light against the ground like playing a game with a cat. Rex knew what he'd do if he was Tip.

The light stops.

"You see something over there?" Jerry asks. Rex watches Tip focus on the ground as if he's about to bend over and examine something.

"Naw," he says, looking directly at Rex. "You find anything on him?"

Jerry gives his head a shake.

"We done then?" Tip asks.

"Yep," Jerry says. Rex put his hands down and feet together. "But write him up since he was doing 92 in a 60. And also, safety neglect, no side mirrors." Rex had taken them off, two pounds apiece. He had learned everything gets faster. Jerry continues, "You're not wearing a helmet. Could get you for reckless driving, but I figure you'll learn that the hard way."

Tip hands Rex the tickets, avoiding eye contact, and walking straight to the vehicle. Jerry lays a hand on the biker's shoulder. "You gotta remember two things, son. One, know where you're going. Two, know you're nothing but 3D. I see you well, real well." He turns his back and walks to the car. "The clock don't stop," Jerry says. "I don't either. I know everything. All these parts."

Rex watches Jerry get behind the wheel. The cops make a U-turn in the road, heading back to where they came from. He rests his right foot on the kick-start. Before putting all of his energy into the kick of his foot, he says, "Don't know shit" in a tone that is as low and silent as the trees are dark. Rex would come back tomorrow. He cranks his bike. It yells like the collapse of a star.

AUTHOR BIOS

PATTI ABBOTT's stories have appeared in more than 100 publications over the last decade. She is the author of *Monkey Justice* (Snubnose Press) and the forthcoming novel in stories, *Home Invasion* (which got its start on Thuglit). She won a Derringer for "My Hero" in 2008. You can find her at http://pattinase.blogspot.com.

ERIC BEETNER is the author of *The Devil Doesn't Want Me*, *Dig Two Graves* and the story collection, *A Bouquet Of Bullets*. He is co-author (with JB Kohl) of the novels *One Too Many Blows To The Head* and *Borrowed Trouble*. He has also written two novellas in the popular Fightcard series, *Split Decision* and *A Mouth Full Of Blood*. His award-winning stories have appeared in over a dozen anthologies and he was voted 2012 Most Criminally Underrated Author by the Stalker Awards. For more visit ericbeetner.blogspot.com

GARRETT CROWE currently lives in Chattanooga, Tennessee. His writing has appeared in several print and online publications. He works in public radio. You can follow him at twitter.com/crowegarrett

ROGER HOBBS graduated from Reed College in Portland, Oregon in 2011. He is the author of *Ghostman*, a heist thriller, out now from Alfred A. Knopf. He is 24 years old

CHRISTOPHER L. IRVIN scribbles about the dark and mysterious and dreams of one day writing full time. His stories have appeared in the University of Maine at Machias Binnacle Ultra Short Competition, Weird Noir, Shotgun Honey and The Rusty Nail Magazine among others. He lives with his wife and son in Boston, Massachusetts. You can find him online at www.HouseLeagueFiction.com

ANTON SIM has wasted several careers in nonfiction scribbling about things that really happened and prefers writing about things that didn't, couldn't, and shouldn't. He is proud to be a Thuglet.

ALBERT TUCHER has published more than forty short stories about prostitute Diana Andrews. She has appeared in *Thuglit*, *DZ Allen's Muzzle Flash*, and the anthology *The Best American Mystery Stories 2010*, edited by Lee Child. Most recently she took on Atlantic City in *The Retro Look*, from Untreed Reads. Albert Tucher will also appear in *Ellery Queen Mystery Magazine* in 2013 with a stand-alone story called *Hangman's Break*. Like so many authors of hardboiled crime fiction, he is a librarian in his day job.

SAM WIEBE's first novel, *Last of the Independents*, won the 2012 Arthur Ellis Award for Best Unpublished First Novel, and will be published by Dundurn in 2013. His stories have been published in Spinetingler and Thousand Islands Life. His story "Humanitarian" won second place in the 2011 Scene of the Crime contest. He lives in Vancouver

TODD ROBINSON (Editor) is the creator and Chief Editor of Thuglit. His writing has appeared in Blood & Tacos, Plots With Guns, Needle Magazine, Shotgun Honey, Strange, Weird, and Wonderful, Out of the Gutter, Pulp Pusher, Grift, Demolition Magazine, CrimeFactory and the anthologies Lost Children: Protectors, and Danger City. He has been nominated for a Derringer Award, short-listed for Best American Mystery Stories, selected for Writers Digest's Year's Best Writing 2003 and won the inaugural Bullet Award in June 2011. The first collection of his short stories, <u>Dirty Words</u> is now available and his debut novel <u>The Hard Bounce</u> is available from Tyrus Books.

ALLISON GLASGOW (Editor) was once the only woman on the Spike's Hot Dogs Wall of Fame (Fall River, MA).

JULIE MCCARRON (Editor) is a celebrity ghostwriter with three New York Times bestsellers to her credit. Her books have appeared on every major entertainment and television talk show; they have been featured in Publishers Weekly and excerpted in numerous magazines including People. Prior to collaborating on celebrity bios, Julie was a book editor for many years. Julie started her career writing press releases and worked in the motion picture publicity department of Paramount Pictures and for Chasen & Company in Los Angeles. She also worked at General Publishing Group in Santa Monica and for the Dijkstra Literary Agency in Del Mar before turning to editing/writing full-time. She lives in Southern California.

Can't wait another two months for more **THUGLIT???**

Check out these titles from THUGLIT contributors.

Available **NOW** from **Tyrus Books**

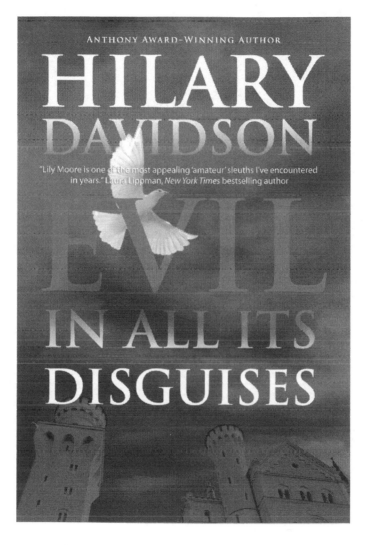

Available March 5, 2013 from **Forge**

Available **NOW** from **Alfred A. Knopf**

THUGLIT

Follow
THUGLIT

on FACEBOOK

or

on TWITTER at:
twitter.com/Thuglit

or just head over to:

Made in the USA
San Bernardino, CA
14 June 2016